BLACK POWDER SHOWDOWN

The gang froze at the sound of Clint Rider's voice, loud in the silence of the street.

"Riney Stark! I have a warrant for the arrest of you and your men, signed by the sheriff of Pinal County, Arizona Territory. Give up and there won't be any trouble."

"You know what you can do with that warrant, marshal," Stark growled, his tenseness evident as he checked his gun, loosening it in the holster.

"I took an oath to uphold the law, Stark."

Riney bowed slightly in acknowledgement. "I'm sorry, then, marshal. Real sorry."

Rider threw the Winchester to his shoulder and fired off a round.

But Riney Stark had moved even faster. . . .

TALES OF THE OLD WEST

SPIRIT WARRIOR (1795, $2.50)
by G. Clifton Wisler
The only settler to survive the savage indian attack was a little boy. Although raised as a red man, every man was his enemy when the two worlds clashed—but he vowed no man would be his equal.

IRON HEART (1736, $2.25)
by Walt Denver
Orphaned by an indian raid, Ben vowed he'd never rest until he'd brought death to the Arapahoes. And it wasn't long before they came to fear the rider of vengeance they called . . . Iron Heart.

WEST OF THE CIMARRON (1681, $2.50)
by G. Clifton Wisler
Eric didn't have a chance revenging his father's death against the Dunstan gang until a stranger with a fast draw and a dark past arrived from West of the Cimarron.

HIGH LINE RIDER (1615, $2.50)
by William A. Lucky
In Guffey Creek, you either lived by the rules made by Judge Breen and his hired guns—or you didn't live at all. So when Holly took sides against the Judge, it looked like there would be just one more body for the buzzards. But this time they were wrong.

GUNSIGHT LODE (1497, $2.25)
by Virgil Hart
When Ned Coffee cornered Glass and Corey in a mine shaft, the last thing Glass expected was for the kid to make a play for the gold. And in a blazing three-way shootout, both Corey and Coffee would discover how lightening quick Glass was with a gun.

Available wherever paperbacks are sold, or order direct from the Publisher. Send cover price plus 50¢ per copy for mailing and handling to Zebra Books, Dept. 1934, 475 Park Avenue South, New York, N.Y. 10016. Residents of New York, New Jersey and Pennsylvania must include sales tax. DO NOT SEND CASH.

GALLOWS RIDERS

BY MARK K. ROBERTS

ZEBRA BOOKS
KENSINGTON PUBLISHING CORP.

ZEBRA BOOKS

are published by

Kensington Publishing Corp.
475 Park Avenue South
New York, NY 10016

Copyright © 1986 by Mark K. Roberts

All rights reserved. No part of this book may be reproduced in any form or by any means without the prior written consent of the Publisher, excepting brief quotes used in reviews.

First printing: November 1986

Printed in the United States of America

Dedicated to Jack Elam, gifted actor and friend, whose zany ideas over screwdrivers at the Inn Between contributed greatly to this story.

MKR

Prologue

First to be distinguished against the widening band of light in the east were the saguaro cacti, their bulky arms raised to the sky like the many pipes of a great organ, the characteristic which gave them their English name. Slowly, the questing fingers of spiky, sausage-thick occotillo resolved into visibility. As yet, not an animal call heralded the coming day. A rag-muffled hoof came into contact with a loose rock, sending up a nearly metallic clatter when the stone skittered away. Instantly the darkness-shrouded line of men froze, ears straining.

"Dang it, Charlie, I told you to be careful." The whispering voice came from the gloom close to the offender's ear.

Moon-faced Charlie Bell grinned ingratiatingly and tried to soften the rebuke by changing the subject. "Riney, you sure these braves are gonna be gone?"

Riney Stark, the leader, grunted softly for an answer and led out his small column of men. Stark had a gaunt, but powerful face, dominant craggy chin and hard, gray eyes. His broad shoulders and trim waist attested to his many hours in the saddle. He'd ridden the owlhoot trail since a few months following Lee's surrender at Appomattox. His survival over the many years served as proof of his qualifications to lead. In turn, he felt confident of his men, though he harbored some reservations about two of them.

Marv Hoyle seemed fast enough with a gun and fair with a knife, but he was young. Too young to be fully trusted operating with the gang. His only credentials for membership consisted of robbing the small bank in his hometown of Colby, New Mexico Territory, killing the teller in the process and managing to evade the posse sent after him. He had a mild, boyish face that reflected innocence, long, slender fingers and, a slight build. At seventeen, he was the youngest in the gang by nearly two decades. Riney had taken Marv in because they needed an extra gun. On the other hand, Charlie Bell had been with the gang for nearly four years.

Trouble was misfortune—or perhaps misadventure, Riney corrected—seemed to ride double-girt with Charlie. Not gifted with even a normal amount of intelligence or common sense, the chubby, pink-cheeked Charlie alternated between an almost puppy-like affability and nearly insane rages and sadistic bloodlust. When given a task to accomplish on his own, Marv entered into it with boylike enthusiasm and energy. If he failed in its accomplishment, it would be from inexperience rather than inability; while Charlie stood a good chance of forgetting what it was he had been sent to do. As a result, they both needed a keeper, Riney acknowledged, but he knew they could carry out this mission with ease. They rounded a bluff and Riney reined in, motioning silently for the others to pass him by. While they did, he examined each in turn.

Abner Perkins, called Perk by all and sundry since his childhood, came first. Perk had served under Riney in the disaster-haunted Army of Tennessee. He had fought well and bravely and wept bitterly when news of the Confederacy's fall reached them. He had gone back to his North Georgia mountain home, only to return some months later to look for Riney Stark amid the charred ruins of the latter's former Atlanta home. Perk looked ravaged, his long, lank body bowed with an inner grief, his once broad shoulders slumped in defeat. He said little, merely that his family lay dead at the hands of the Yankees. He and Riney formed a partnership, vowing to forge a better life in the free lands to the west, far beyond the civilized barbarities of Yankee occupation and Reconstruction.

Next in line came Pearly Wilson. George Thurmon Wilson, III, carried the manners and speech patterns of Boston with him like a cloak of shabby respectability. He had ridden with Riney and Perk for five years, since that day when the two men had found themselves pinned down by the guns of an angry posse, in a draw a day's ride from Lemar, Colorado. Suddenly, when Riney felt sure their days were numbered by only the time it would take to tie a hangman's knot, the lawmen sprang from their cover behind rocks and raced for their horses, routed by an unexpected attack from behind.

Both outlaws rose to send a fusillade whining after the retreating backs of the posse. While the figures dwindled in the distance, they waited and watched a single man ride toward them. Introductions were sparingly made and, when asked why he had put in his hand, Pearly replied that he had little love for lawmen.

"Never could countenance them. Bloody corrupt lot most I've known." From that day forward, the Riney Stark gang numbered three.

Behind Pearly came Charlie Bell with Marv Hoyle bringing up the rear, leading two pack horses. Satisfied, Riney mounted and rode slowly to the head of the line. More light filled the sky, an orange sliver of sun breaking over the distant ridge. It turned to ruddy life the thrusting column of a mesa in the near distance. Riney rode toward it and the figure of another man heading their way. Behind him the others mounted and urged their horses into a slow lope.

Wind fluttered the fringes of Riney's buckskin jacket, and the growing morning let him clearly see the worn butternut trousers of linsey-woolsey material with their age-frayed and faded yellow stripe along the seam. He pulled his battered gray hat low on his head and reined in beside the newcomer.

"Well, Davey?" Riney dismounted while they waited for the others to arrive.

Davey Two-Knife only nodded in the affirmative for an answer. He sat astride his piebald gelding with his arms crossed, thick, strong fingers clutching bulging biceps. He wore soft, pliable leather trousers, sewn with rawhide and sinew, his barrel chest covered by a light-weight, gaudy flannel shirt. Davey's long black hair was held back by a calico bandana. A wide beaded belt spanned his narrow-waisted middle, and tucked into it across the front was a bulky Colt's Dragoon pistol. Two knives, a thick-bladed bowie and slender skinner, hung suspended from the belt in bead-decorated sheaths. Davey's hawk-bill nose and high cheekbones seemed out of place in a face dominated by a thin-lipped mouth and eyes of a decidedly Anglo cast and color. The coppery glow of his skin, though, left no doubt as to his half-Indian ancestry.

When the others arrived, Riney remounted and turned to his men. "It's just like we expected, boys. Let's ride . . . and keep quiet." Riney drew a Henry repeating rifle from his saddle scabbard, nosed his mount around and started into the wide, rubble-strewn canyon that provided access to the mesa top. Davey pulled a heavy Spencer carbine, rested it across his muscular thighs, and fell into line beside Riney. The other four paired up and followed.

Darkness claimed them again when they went further between the steep walls of the cut. The floor, strewn with rocks and powdery soil from countless centuries of erosion, further muffled their hoofbeats. For five minutes they continued while the canyon sides closed in on them and the over-hanging rim nearly blotted out all light. At a curt nod from Davey Two-Knife, Riney raised his hand in the universal signal to halt. The riders dismounted and securely tied their horses. Spreading out into a skirmish line, they began a long, silent climb to the top.

Chapter 1

Tis-natan liked the Sun Returning part of the day best of all. Particularly with the men who had gone hunting it gave a special importance to the coming of the new day. That meant that only he and the other boys of the *rancheria* were up and stirring. *Tis-natan* smiled with satisfaction over this as he crawled from the *wikiup* and stood stretching the night's sleep from his small, supple limbs.

Then he replaced the circular brush cover in the low, round opening. Thrusting his arms above his head, he wriggled his entire body delightedly, enjoying the sensation of awakening muscles. That accomplished he bent to slip on a pair of high-topped moccasins and, with legs far astraddle, drew on a breechcloth. He carefully adjusted it through the braided cord that circled his slender waist so that it hung to his knees front and rear.

This final act brought him the greatest pleasure of all. Only when the men and older youths were off on the hunt or a war party were the boys of the *rancheria* entitled to wear the symbols of manhood. Those who owned less than twelve summers went entirely naked through their days, save for a pair of low-topped moccasins and the braided rawhide belt, with a warm, loose-fitting shift for the Moon of Frozen Rain. Now, though, they defended, if only symbolically, the village and as such were allowed to dress the part of men. Thrusting out his skinny chest and buttocks, *Tis-natan* tried to duplicate the pigeon-toed, arrogant strut of a warrior as he walked toward the mesa rim where it was split by the canyon that provided access to their *rancheria*. From the corner of his eye he caught sight of his best friend, *Honapi Taksin*.

"*Hoa!* Sleeping Owl. You are living up to your name with those puffy eyes. Come, let us greet the new day with our prayers . . . if you are not too sleepy to remember the words."

Sleeping Owl finished adjusting his breechcloth and sprinted to join his friend. Small white teeth gleamed in his wide-mouthed grin. "*He yata-no, yata he,*" he greeted both the coming day and his companion. "You are a fine one to talk. Look, the sleep pebbles still cluster in your eyes."

Tis-natan raised small fists and knuckled the grains from his eyes. That completed, he broke into a lope, calling back to his friend.

"Hurry! I feel like a mighty river has been trapped inside me. I must let it out, then we will pray to our grandfather, the sun, and run to the mountain."

"Must we? Why should we run when there is no one here to make us?"

Tis-natan laughed derisively at his friend. "You will grow fat as well as lazy and waddle around like an old woman, Sleeping Owl. Come. It is a beautiful new day!" *Tis-natan* circled back to push playfully at his companion's chest.

Sleeping Owl shoved back and broke into a shuffle. Both boys continued to pummel each other as they neared the canyon edge. When they reached the rim, they drew aside their breechcloths. Careful not to select the hand used for eating, each boy clutched his small penis and directed an arching golden stream of urine over the side into space. Giggling, they compared the length, force, and duration of their efforts. To the Apache, and most Indians untouched by the white man's ways, the body and all its parts were subjects of great humor. Behind the youngsters, other boys came from their *wikiups* to engage in the same rituals.

Careful not to make the least sound, Charlie Bell and Davey Two-Knife crawled slowly on all fours until they reached the top of the canyon walk a little ahead of the others. Cautiously they brought their eyes up over the rim.

Fifty yards away, coming directly toward them, were two Apache boys. They looked to be about ten years old. They were busy teasing each other, trotting with loose-limbed grace while they aimed light, playful blows at back and shoulders. Davey and Charlie dropped quickly back out of sight.

"Damn, where are the others?" Charlie whispered querulously.

"Shush," Davey cautioned. Davey drew his knife and crouched to spring. His sharp ears heard the boys reach the canyon rim and pause. Then twin sparkling streams descended, striking the ground near the hidden men. Splatters of warm urine hit on a rock near Charlie and splashed onto his face. He stifled a curse and looked around to see the remaining men moving into place. He gave Davey a nod, and they both sprang swiftly upward.

Rising in a blur, Davey grabbed one small boy and thrust his knife deep into the wriggling child's abdomen, pushing upward to pierce the diaphragm. Beside him, Charlie tripped over a rock and fell on his face at the feet of the second youngster.

In the same instant, *Tis-natan* overcame the immobility of his shock and surprise. Whirling, he began to run at full speed toward the *rancheria* and yelled a warning:

"*Pelegro! Pelegro! Quidado, los Pen-dik-olye!* White-eye devils are coming."

Behind the fleeing boy, Davey dropped the small corpse he held by one shoulder and pulled free his knife, drops of blood flying from its blade as he drew back his arm and threw it toward the other Apache child. The shining steel went true, sinking its keenly sharp tip and edge to the hilt in *Tis-natan*'s back, slipping between two ribs to pierce his heart. The boy's cry of warning choked off in a gurgling shriek, and *Tis-natan* fell dead. To both sides, Davey heard the popping reports of revolvers as the others joined the fray.

Riney Stark, a smoking Navy Colt in each hand, rushed forward, the others on his heels. The people of the Apache village were still drugged with sleep as they crawled from their *wikiups*, women calling shrilly to each other, asking what was happening. Bullets and balls sang in the air, and two half-dressed young squaws fell in boneless heaps in the entrance to their dwellings. Charlie had regained his feet and lumbered heavily after the attackers, spotting an old man who crouched in the low opening of a *wikiup* to aim a bow at Riney.

The arrow fell far short of its target. Quickly the ancient Apache plucked another from his quiver but failed to discharge it. Charlie's .44 slug caught the oldster in the side of his head, splashing his *wikiup* with blood as he fell dead. With fierce yells, the men charged on until they reached the far end.

"Okay. Split up and fan out through the village. Get them all." Riney followed his own command, turning to his left and stalking deliberately toward the nearest *wikiup*. He fired three times through the brush entrance cover, a grimace of satisfaction on his face at the sound of death throes coming from inside. Each of his henchmen pursued his own grim course while Riney holstered one revolver and drew a pre-loaded cylinder from a leather pouch on his belt to replace the empty one in his .36 caliber Colt.

Trembling with fear, but determined to be as brave and fierce as warriors, Bear-Runs-At-Sky and his twin brother, Second-Bear-Cub, pressed their backs against the outer wall of their family's *wikiup*, arrows nocked to their small rabbit bows, waiting The two naked eleven-year-olds had not come from their sleeping place for the morning ritual when the attack began. Still flushed with the warmth of slumber, they listened in disbelief to *Tis-natan*'s wild cry, followed by gunshots and screams. They grabbed the only weapons at hand and made ready to fight for their *rancheria*. Now they heard the flat reports of detonating revolvers and the screams of the dying and wounded draw ever nearer. Tenseness filled them as they drew back their bows and got ready to make a rush into the fight. Suddenly the shadow of a hated white-eye darkened the ground inside the entrance, and their ears rang with thunder and noses tingled with powder smoke while a big Remington .44 blasted into the brush lodge.

Perk Perkins spun to his left and shot into the next *wikiup* in line. Hearing no response, he stooped low and entered. True to habit he spoke to himself while he undertook the risky task.

"Dang. Now I gotta dig 'em outta there. A feller could get hurt that way."

Perk entered the gloomy interior, his constricted pupils momentarily blinded by the outer brightness. He missed seeing the two small boys pressed to the wall at each side of the opening. When his eyes adjusted he stepped fully into the center of the dwelling and caught sight of an aged, gray-haired woman, crouched fearfully in a pile of animal hides at the rear. Raising his revolver, Perk shot her between the eyes. In the same instant, Bear-Runs-At-Sky and Second-Bear-Cub fired their missiles.

A surprised yelp of pain ripped from Perk's mouth when one small arrow buried its flint tip in the flesh at the back of his right thigh, dangling there, pointing to the ground behind him. The second bolt smacked into the thick leather of his gun belt and clung a moment before falling to the dust. Perk whirled about and, for the first time, saw the young defenders. He swung the muzzle of the big. .44 Army into line and shot down Bear-Runs-At-Sky. Then he turned toward Second-Bear-Cub, who struggled to nock another arrow.

For a moment Perk thought his eyes played tricks on him. This was the same boy he'd just shot. How could that be? Then he realized he had come upon a rare instance among Indians: twins. In the moment while he wondered over this, Second-Bear-Cub gave up the attempt of his fear-numbed fingers at fitting arrow to string and threw aside his bow. He drew his knife and leaped at Perk, snarling in soprano viciousness.

Perk's left arm shot out, knocking the knife thrust away. He grabbed the small boy by one shoulder and began shaking him like a terrier worrying a rabbit. Struggling furiously, the little Apache tried to slash Perk's brawny arm with the blade he still clutched in his tiny fist. Perk swung his revolver in a slow arc, smacking its heavy barrel into the side of the boy's head.

When Second-Bear-Cub slumped in Perk's grasp, the outlaw rearranged his hold, closed his huge hand around the slender youngster's throat and squeezed tightly. While Perk increased the pressure, the small bronze figure's struggles became more and more feeble. The boy's face turned purple-black. His eyes bulged and his tongue protruded from his mouth, past peeled-back lips. At last he convulsed violently and went limp.

A final death spasm brought Second-Bear-Cub's hand around with enough force so that his razor-edged hunting knife bit into skin and flesh. Perk grunted in irritation when blood welled from the shallow cut on his arm. He threw aside the dead child and stooped to leave the *wikiup*, wincing at the pain in the back of his right thigh.

Outside, Charlie Bell grinned hugely while he attached a scalp-lock to his belt, secure among several others. Wet, red stains widened on his trousers. Chuckling maniacally, he headed toward another dead Apache woman.

" 'Nother 'dobe dollar made," Charlie chortled aloud. "Hey, Marv, how you doin'?"

Marv Holye looked a bit green around the gills. Yet he had the wild, twisted gleam of an icy killer glowing in his eyes. He rose from the ground where he had just scalped a small girl. His collarless and cuffless white shirt was splattered with crimson, its lace front looking even more out of place with greasy smudges of burned black powder that showed clear evidence of his eager participation. He wiped a bloodstained hand on his whipcord trousers before he made a reply:

" 'Bout as good as you, Charlie. Got me three o' these 'Pache scalps. Goin' for more. You with me?"

"You bet! This is more fun than the parson's picnic."

The two men turned away to pursue their grisly task as Riney Stark came around the edge of a smoldering *wikiup*, inspecting a shiny new Winchester Model '73 repeating rifle. Greasy powder stains smudged his face, and his interest in the new weapon was obvious. He nearly bumped into Pearly as he veered suddenly to the right. Behind the two men another *wikiup* burst into flame.

"Oh, sorry, Pearly. You got a minute?"

"I reckon so. What is it?"

"Take a look at this."

Pearly's eyes went to the new rifle in his leader's hands. He pursed his lips and whistled in admiration. "Man alive, lookie at that. Heard Winchester weren't puttin' them out yet."

Riney hefted his newly acquired firearm again. He tested the action, sighted along the barrel. "Marv tole me they had a few for sale in St. Louis last time he was there. Sure is a nice one."

"Trust the damned Comancheros to get their hands on 'em first and sell 'em to the Injuns before us decent folk have them," Pearly said bitterly.

They continued to admire the rifle for several seconds. A female scream came from one distant *wikiup*, followed by Davey's bitter laughter. The two men turned from their examination of the gun to watch the byplay.

Suddenly the girl darted out the opening to the *wikiup* and ran directly toward Riney and Pearly. She looked over her shoulder, oblivious to all around her, in her attempt to escape. From where he stood, Riney could see a thin film of blood running down her forehead. Behind her, Davey Two-Knife crawled out of the brush shelter and rose to his feet, to stand spread legged. He held his scalping knife in one hand, a .44 Colt Dragoon in the other. Through his bellowing laughter, he yelled to the others:

"Can't understand women. She didn't like the idea of gettin' scalped." With a rapid change of mood, his laughter ended.

A look of utter concentration came over Davey's face, and he took slow, almost careless aim at the young Apache. A suspended fraction of a second passed and he fired.

The big bullet smacked into her flesh between the shoulder blades. Force of the impact caused the Apache woman to stumble. Her eyes went wide with fright and shock, then they glazed over as she fell face forward in the dirt, almost at Riney's feet. Davey crossed to her and kneeled down, his scalping knife ready.

"Damn it, Davey," Riney growled. "I was right in the line of fire."

"I didn't hit you, did I?" came the casual reply.

Pearly's indifference to the hideous carnage they had created added a nightmarish unreality to the unspeakable activities. "How much you figger we'll make off these scalps, Riney?"

"Mezkins payin' five dollars gold for each 'Pache scalp brought in. They ain't particular iffin they's kids scalps or no. With all the brats in this *rancheria* we should realize several hundred dollars."

"It's like that yeller-hair horse soldier we ran into up in Nebraska said, eh?"

"Custer? Yeah. 'Nits make lice.' I figger the Mezkins agree with him. You want to get rid of Injuns, you stamp out the next generation. Let's get it over with."

Riney lit a brush torch and applied it to the nearest *wikiup*. An innate fastidiousness, left over from his genteel antebellum past, made Riney refrain from participating in taking scalps. But over the next few minutes, he fired five *wikiups* and shot three wounded survivors. When he neared a sixth brush lodge, a child's scream came from inside.

The shriek turned to a moan of pain, which continued while Charlie walked out through the entranceway toward Riney and Pearly. Blood still dripped from a small, fresh scalp, which he tucked in his belt. He wiped his bloody hands on his homespun trousers, then took a sack of tobacco from the pocket of his Mexican cactus fiber vest. From the sweatband of his stained and battered tall-crowned hat he took a match and scratched it to life with one grimy, broken thumbnail. He touched the flame to the twisted end of the cigarette he'd hurriedly rolled and took a deep drag.

"Found me a smart li'l feller. He was playin' possum. Littly bitty kid, about so high." Charlie indicated size with a hand at his waist, in front of his paunchy belly. "I didn't know it until I started to scalp the li'l devil. He shore let out a beller." Charlie guffawed at his own gallows humor, smoke spouting from nose and mouth, though the others remained silent. Charlie took another drag on his cigarette, then threw it down when Perk Perkins came toward them, limping heavily.

"What happened, Perk?"

Perk felt chagrin at the way he had received his wound. What he did not need was a razzing from Charlie Bell. He cast a baleful glare at the fat outlaw while answering Riney's question. "Aw, Riney, it was one of them li'l uns. He an' his, by God, twin brother tried to ambush me. Shot me with this." Perk produced the child's small rabbit arrow, about twenty inches long, with a crudely made point, which held only a slight strain of dried blood. At sight of it, Charlie began giggling insanely.

"It ain't *that* funny, Charlie, dang it. Hell, if it weren't fer these leather britches, this li'l thing would of gone right deep into my leg. So, I'll thank you, Mr. Charlie Bell Mushhead to keep yer fool giggling to yerself." Perk's glance took in the dripping trophies at Charlie's bulging waist, and his mood changed. "How many did we get?"

"Sixty, near's I figger," Riney told him.

Perk whistled appreciatively, calculating in his head the value there. "Why, Riney, that makes nigh onto three hundred dollars in gold."

Pearly strode to a *wikiup*, which shimmered in its consuming flames. He took careful aim and kicked the remaining support pole, letting the brush shelter crash in on itself. "Where d'we cash 'em in?"

Riney gestured toward the south, to where the desert of Mexico flickered in the increasing heat of midmorning. Close by, Marv and Davey finished up the last of the scalpings. Davey looked around and, satisfied they had nothing more to do, motioned toward the canyon rim.

"Go bring the *caballos*, kid."

A look of rebelliousness flashed across Marv's face, heralding a beginning protest. Davey's brows knotted together in an angry frown. At sight of this ominous warning, Marv hastily moderated his mood. "Aw . . . okay, sure, Davey."

Rising, head down and lips set in stubborn resentment, Marv walked past the others and disappeared over the lip of the mesa. The others went about their business as though the little scene had not occurred.

"Riney's got him a place, Pearly. Right over the border there's a Mezkin town. Place called Nogales. The army there is payin' hard money for this bristly hair."

"That's right, Charlie. And Nogales is on the way to where we hit that silver shipment. Now let's clear outta here. Might be these fires will draw back some of them braves."

With a nod of agreement, the gang turned as one and walked toward the narrow trail leading down into the canyon, from where they could hear the sound of approaching horses.

Another fine day's work done, Riney thought with satisfaction.

Chapter 2

Deep worry creases seamed *Natana-jo*'s forehead. He had been considering the possible meaning of the rising columns of smoke he and his hunters had spotted early that morning. They came from the approximate location of the *rancheria*.

Could it be that the hated *Me-ji-kanos* had violated the white-eye invisible fence again and attacked the village? Or perhaps those old women Navajos had mustered enough courage to send out a war party after that raid he had led against them during the Moon of Frozen Rain? *Natana-jo*'s thoughts stopped as he saw the flickering mirror signal of their scout. He drummed heels into his horse's ribs and hurried forward.

"What is it?" *Natana-jo* asked when he halted beside the scout who waited below the crest of the next ridge.

For answer the scout pointed silently in the direction of the crest and beyond to the unseen mesa the tribe called their home. Silently the two men made their way through the screen of trees on the reverse slope until they could clearly see the tall butte, with its shadowed cleft of canyon. *Natana-jo* felt a rising sickness and anger in his stomach when he looked across the five miles that separated him from the *rancheria*.

"Many fires?"

"*He-yah.*" The scout made the hand sign for three fives, then repeated it—the same number as lodges in their village. "Whoever did it is gone. We can ride in openly."

Natana-jo signaled the others, and they all lashed their ponies into a furious run. Their horses foamed and glistened with sweat when they entered the canyon floor half an hour later. Each man's mouth was set in a grim line, eyes hooded. *Natana-jo* took the lead, climbing the narrow trail at a pace dangerously fast for his mount.

Twenty Apache warriors rode over the rim of the canyon, onto the flat-topped mesa that had been their home. Although they came closest to the white man's false stereotype of the blank-faced, unfeeling Indian, the Apache could show emotion readily. The hunters' faces registered shock and grief when they looked at the smoldering ruins of their village. One after another they took up a howl of mourning as their eyes rested everywhere upon crumpled heaps—the bodies of their families, relatives, and friends, covered with industrious ants and flies, bodies already bloating in the heat of late afternoon. Dismounting, they went among the dead, identifying loved ones. *Natana-jo* took several tottering, uncertain steps toward two small bronze bodies nearest the canyon edge.

"*Tis-natan! Tis-natan!*" *Natana-jo*'s grief wailed out in chest-heaving sobs when he knelt beside the corpse of his only son. Gently he lifted the lifeless boy in his arms and stumbled on toward the heap of ashes that had been his *wikiup*. There, in its ruins, he found the blackened lumps that were his two young wives and three daughters. Dropping to his knees he gave full rein to his awful sorrow.

All around him, the warriors voiced their own anguished bereavement, the enormous success of their three day hunt entirely forgotten. Rocking on their heels, the braves alternately struck the ground and their bare chests, singing the death song for all their lost family and friends, naming each one and commending their spirits to the Sky God. The men slashed off ragged hunks of their hair and cut shallow gashes in their arms to give vent to their sorrow. The loud, violent mourning went on for over an hour. At last, *Natana-jo* rose, smeared his face with ashes and raised his arms above his head to summon his men.

The war chief struggled to control his voice. "Look for tracks. We will find these men and avenge our people."

Several warriors hurried to obey, searching among the burned mounds of the *wikiups* and over the mesa top. One man went to the trail leading down the canyon. In a few moments he and the others returned.

"They were white men. Many boot tracks on ground."

"Your eyes see truth, *Kakka-pey*." *Natana-jo* looked at the others. "What else do you see?"

"They left by way of the canyon."

"An obvious observation, foolish *Tamka*. How else would they go? Can men fly?"

The boy, youngest of the hunting party, flushed and lowered his head at this not entirely gentle rebuke. Then he brightened and headed for his horse. "I will ride down and see which way they went on the desert floor. I will be able to easily tell, for their horses will have the iron feet."

"Good boy. Now you use the mind the Great Spirit gave you." *Tamka* rode swiftly, warmed by this sign of his leader's approval. *Natana-jo* turned to instruct his men.

"It is too late to track these white devils today. We must care for our dead and see them properly mourned. As of this day we are no longer a clan of the People. Our women, children, old ones . . . all are dead . . . and we are men without a home . . . renegades! So then we will act like renegades, killing all who get in our way. For with tomorrow's sun we shall ride after those who did this. We will find them. And when we do, not one of them shall live. This I vow."

Heat waves shimmered off the whitewashed adobe walls of the buildings in Nogales, Sonora, while Riney Stark and his gang rode through the afternoon heat toward the high palisade of the small fort at the far edge of town. When they neared the village, not a sign of human habitation could be seen. The outlaws bunched together, reining in.

"Well, there it is. Nogales," Riney announced.

"Not what you'd call an impressive town," Pearly opined.

"Yep. But gold's gold wherever you find it. Let's get out of this heat." Riney spurred his mount, taking the lead as the others strung out behind him.

In a few moments they had entered the dusty main street. Low, flat-roofed houses lined both sides, giving way a block further to the central plaza, with its inevitable church, fountain, *Edificio Municipal, mercado*, and a trio of cantinas. They still saw no signs of life. Even the Mexican flags on staffs before the municipal offices and jail and above the distant wall of the military compound hung limply in the still, burning air. The sudden yapping of a scruffy yellow dog so startled Charlie that he let out a yelp of his own and drew his revolver.

"Dang mutt," Charlie grumbled when the others laughed at his edginess. He worked the thick wad of chewing tobacco in his mouth and squirted a long brown stream toward the pooch. The offended animal rushed to cover inside the dark, shadowed entrance to an adobe house.

"That's showin' him, Charlie," Perk cackled.

The small column of six men split around the central fountain in the plaza and continued on toward the buff-colored walls of the fort. When they neared they could see the bulky form of a sentry on the parapet, slouched in the sparse shade of the higher gate posts. Once the riders reached the closed portal, they halted their horses. Riney raised his right hand in the universal sign of peace.

"Hola, Señor Cabo! Queremos permiso de la fortaleza de entrada, por favor."

Snorting, the guard jerked suddenly erect, startled awake by the sound of Riney's voice asking for the gate to be opened. He clenched the stub of a small black cigar in his large, yellowed teeth. "Ah, *señores*. I am only a lowly private soldier, not a corporal. Why is it you wish the entrance to our fort?"

"We have business with the *comandante*, concerning

the bounty offered."

"*Ay, sí!*" the guard interrupted. "For the scalps of the *Indios, verdad?*" He turned away and bellowed. "Corporal of the guard, Post Number Two! Open the gate!"

When the double wings of trimmed piñon pines swung wide, Riney and Davey entered and tied their mounts on the shady side of the compound. The others remained outside. Riney and Davey headed across the hard-packed dirt parade ground, carrying with them a large burlap sack that bulged with its grim load. Perk, Charlie, Pearly, and Marv lounged against the outer wall. Bored, Marv began to play a game of mumble-the-peg. Feeling superior to such childish pursuits, the others ignored him.

Near the commandant's office, Riney and Davey paused long enough to wash off some of the trail dust in a basin of water, provided for that purpose. Once they had wiped their faces dry with bandanas and slicked back their damp hair, both outlaws refreshed themselves with deep drinks out of a dipper taken from a handy bucket.

"Sure is nice of these Mezkins to provide for us like this, Davey."

"It's only because the *comandante* figgers he's too good to have to talk with dirty people. Ever'body's expected to wash off before they can go inside, even if it's an emergency. Fancy fellers these post *comandantes*. Lots of lace and gaudy uniforms. But I'll bet you ten dollars he's no more than a captain. Let's git our business out of the way so's we can have some grub and do a little serious drinkin'."

They used their hats to knock dust from their clothes, then entered the cool, darkened interior. A clerk looked up inquisitively, abandoning the paperwork he had been occupied with. His uniform was worn and wrinkled, but he had about him an air of efficiency.

"*Buenas tardes, señores. Que queres?*"

"*Muy buenas, Señor Cabo. Es el capitan aqui?*" Davey hefted the bag of scalps to indicate their business with the commandant, all the while giving a knowing look to Riney. A captain it was. He had won his bet.

The clerk's eyes glowed with pleasure. "*Tenen pericarneos? Bueno. El comandante es por aja in la oficina. Major Gonzales. Entradarse, por favor.*"

Major Gonzales! Riney smirked at Davey, who turned to him to translate, forgetting Riney spoke as good or better Spanish than himself. As the clerk turned back to his paperwork, Riney extended a hand. "*Major* Gonzales, eh? Pay me."

Davey frowned and pushed his lips out into a near pout. He dug into his pocket for a gold piece while they walked to the door and knocked.

Charlie and the others climbed expectantly to their feet when Riney and Davey came out of the gate, their horses led behind them. Riney fingered stacks of gold coins while the others anxiously crowded around them. Avarice turned Charlie's face into the likeness of a ruddy-cheeked, ugly cherub.

"All right, all right! Everybody'll get his right now. We had sixty scalps. That was good for three hundred in gold. And we told the comandante we wiped out a whole village."

"That brought a bonus," Davey interrupted. "We got

five dollars each from the scalps and two dollars, four bits each for a bonus. That made a total of four hundred fifty."

Perk let out a whoop of pure animal joy. "Let's head for that cantina yonder."

"Me for some food." Charlie rubbed his fat belly to emphasize his need.

Pearly stroked his moustache, eyes atwinkle, a look of lecherous anticipation lighting his face. "Now me, I'll take the *mujeres*."

Suddenly the joking ended and the men pressed close on Riney, their hands out for their share. "Now just hold on a minute. We set out to do one particular job, right? We've got to be in Montenegro by late afternoon day after tomorrow. Once we've relieved that escort of the silver shipment, we ride for Colby. We can't afford to do any relaxin' until we get there. So I don't want to see any of you go out gettin' drunked up, locked in that jail over there or hung up with some woman. You all got that?"

A ripple of nods went around the clustered outlaws, signifying their grudging agreement. Then they pressed close again, hands extended once more. Riney began counting out the gold coins.

"There you go, Pearly. Now you, Charlie." Riney continued counting fifty dollars' value in Mexican gold pieces to each man, handing the last set to Marv.

"We can get change in the cantina, and you'll have your other ten then."

"Ten? What's he mean, ten dollars? Four hundred fifty split six ways is seventy-five each, Pearly."

"He's the leader, Marv. Riney gets the lion's share."

"That's not fair."

"You fixin' to ride out on your own?"

A sullen expression clouded Marv's young face. "No. I'll stick, but it still ain't fair."

Perk dropped several coins into the pudgy hand of the bartender. "There you go, my friend, now just bring them drinks over to our table." He strode across the sawdust-strewn, pounded earth floor to a large, rustic table where the rest of the gang sat. The interior adobe walls of the cantina had been crudely plastered over and given an indifferent coat of cheap whitewash. Posters dotted the walls, advertising past and future bullfights. A pair of well-used guitars hung over a small stage at one side, and an odor of tequila, stale beer, and urine permeated the air. It was, Perk decided, a right passable saloon.

"Drinks are on their way, fellers."

"Sit down, Perk." Riney turned to the others. "Now, remember what I said. Don't go getting boozed up."

Pearly nodded solemnly, his eyes and attention on a scantily clad young woman leaning indolently against one corner of the bar. He licked his lips in appreciation of her ample endowments, face alight with lust. Davey felt moved to protest Riney's restrictions.

"I can understand about stayin' sober until we get that silver and ride on to Colby, Riney. But, dang it, what's so all fired important about Colby?"

Before Riney could reply, the bartender came to their table, his colorful red, white, and green serving tray loaded with shots of tequila, a plate of lemon wedges, and a bowl of salt. He sat the potables in front of everyone, then stood back waiting further instructions.

Perk lifted his glass, disdaining condiments, and knocked the liquor back in a single gulp. Marv followed suit. A gasp escaped him in mid-swallow, and he began to choke, eyes watering. The others sipped at their drinks, chuckling at Marv's difficulty. Marv gusted out a long breath, took a belated bite of lemon and turned to the barkeep, struggling to regain his dignity.

"*El otro, cantinero.*" Marv waved his arm to indicate a round for the table.

"*Sí, señor.*" The bartender rushed to obey the handsome, but evil-looking youth. Charlie looked up at Marv with surprise.

"Where'd you learn their lingo, kid?"

"I told you, Charlie, that we have a lot of Mexes in Colby. In those parts a fella's got to learn Spanish in self-defense." The proprietor returned with their drinks, placed them on the table and collected from Marv.

"There you go about Colby again. What makes it so darn special?"

"I suppose Marv should be the one to explain, Charlie."

Marv responded to Riney's prompting. "Well, boys, what can I tell you? Colby is sort of like any town. It's got a bank, a couple of saloons, a general mercantile, stage line office, and two churches. It also has a city building where the marshal hangs out. Colby is . . . just Colby."

Chapter 3

To be town marshal of Colby, New Mexico Territory, represented quite a comedown for a former Indian fighter and civilian scout for the U.S. Cavalry. At forty-two years of age, his thick shock of soft brown hair and walrus moustache shot through with strands of gray, Clint Rider felt no resentment at his change in status. In fact, he felt downright contented. Although always considered by other men to be tough and courageous, as only a man absolutely convinced of his rightness in every decision and willing to back it up, Clint prided himself in being smart enough to know when it was time to get out. That time had come three years before.

When the offer to become town marshal had been made by the mayor and town counsel, Clint thought it over for a day and replied in the affirmative. Since then he had let out two notches in his belt, and his gun hand had lost some of its former lightning fastness. Yet, Clint represented a formidable force for law and order over the local cowhands and occasional drifter who decided to raise a little unauthorized hell in the dusty streets of Colby. In all, his life had taken on new meaning. For the first time in his memory, he had roots. This was his town and he policed it with stern fairness.

Clint made two rounds during the day, then surrendered his post to young Billy Ash at sunset. If trouble came, Billy had strict instructions to come to the small house where Clay lived alone and rouse the sleeping marshal. Clay didn't believe in asking an untried youngster to do something he wouldn't himself do willingly. It made for a good relationship between the marshal and his deputy. Clay felt an almost paternal warmth and affection for his youthful apprentice. He would, he realized as he sighted the lowering sun, soon be entrusting the town to the boy once again. Smiling, Clay strode across the boardwalk in front of the marshal's office, avoided a mud puddle between a horse trough and the tie rail, and down Main Street toward the general mercantile as Howie and Amy Wilkins came out the door.

"Evenin', Howie . . . ma'am. Pass a peaceable day?"

"Evenin', marshal. That we did."

"Good evening, Marshal Rider." Amy Wilkins's voice carried a coolness, just short of forbidding.

A good-looking woman, Clint Rider thought to himself for perhaps the two thousandth time. Nice figure, if not confined in those severe clothes. Taffy-colored hair, better suited for swinging free about her small, creamy shoulders instead of being confined in that tight bun. But her no-nonsense attitude was exactly what Howie needed.

Howie, the marshal conceded after three years of close friendship, had to have someone to urge him forward. His dreamy approach to life far better suited the settled East than this burr-edged town in a wild and empty land. How could such a delicate and seemingly unworldly an innocent have been born son to so gusty and forceful a frontiersman as the former U.S. marshal, Mason Wilkins? Howie, Clint thought with a hint of regret, resembled his mother in more than physical appearance. Suddenly he realized he had been standing silently, failing to make reply to Amy's question.

"Uh . . . that's right, ma'am. Business good today?"

"Why—" Howie stopped abruptly, interrupted by his wife. He felt a burning embarrassment that his friend had been caught in a trap of his own making.

"Business, as I just finished telling you, marshal, is hardly what it should be." Amy's icy tones subsided while Clint Rider's sun-darkened face flushed crimson, and he gnawed on one corner of his moustache. "Although the midday heat this time of year doesn't favor travel. Surely after the fall rains we can expect an increase in customers."

"Indeed!" Clint seized upon her withdrawal from verbal combat. "Yes, indeed, ma'am. Think we'll get a break in this heat, Howie," Clint studied the sky.

Howie removed his hat and peered upward also, as though to seek auguries in the deepening blue. "Don't know. Sure do hope so."

"So do I. Checkers tonight, Howie?"

"Checkers it is, Clint. Say . . ." Howie stole a peek at his wife's face, finding no enlightenment there. "Oh, eight o'clock at your place?"

"Fine . . . fine. Have a peaceable night, Howie . . . ma'am." Clint tipped his hat respectfully and strolled down the boardwalk to the corner, heading toward the cafe where Billy Ash would be having his evening meal.

"How-ard? Does that man deliberately try to be dull?"

Disappointment rather than anger filled Howie Wilkins's face. His soft brown, spaniel's eyes reflected his mood. "Amy, that's not being at all charitable. Clint isn't used to social exchanges. His years as a frontiersman gave him little opportunity for polite conversation. Please be patient with him. He was a friend of my father's. He's trying his best to . . . adjust."

"As I oftimes wish you would do. Four years at Yale hardly prepared you for life in this . . ." Amy broke off, returning to her second most favorite theme: the failings of Clint Rider. "After three years, one would expect . . . never mind, though. For some men, some things are just . . . not possible." Amy took in the expression on her husband's face and rearranged her features into a conciliatory expression. "I'm sorry, Howard. I shouldn't carry on like that. I realize he is your friend. Your *only* friend in this sorry community, I might add."

Howie's look dissolved into resignation. "Don't start in on Colby again, my dear. Perhaps we should have never come out here, should have taken your father's advice about joining his firm."

Amy sighed. She had won, as usual, but the victory hardly satisfied her. She suddenly felt like making up. "No, Howard. This is your home. You were right in returning. Come along. I'm fixing pork chops for supper."

"With fried potatoes and onions?" Howie sounded pleasantly expectant.

"If you like, dear."

A little after nine o'clock, when Clint and Howie had started on their third game of checkers, the score tied one to one, Billy Ash began his second round of the town. He paused to shake closed doors and peer into darkened windows. All seemed secure. Music tinkled from an out-of-tune piano in Cactus Jack's Idle Time Saloon, an equally off-key chorus of male voices singing the words to a mournful melody about a cowboy who had taken his last long trail ride to the sky. Billy glanced through the bat wings and grinned indulgently. Local boys. No trouble there. He moved on.

From down the street the flat reports of gunfire jerked the youthful deputy to tingling alertness. Hurrying, he clumped down the boardwalk toward the light spilling from the Golden Horn, Colby's only other saloon. Coming from inside, Billy heard the frightened squeals of saloon girls, followed by two more shots. Haste spurred him on, one hand tightly holding the butt of his Remington .44, the one with the conversion cylinder for metallic cartridges that Clint had given him when he signed on as night marshal.

Billy slowed his pace when he reached the door and he cautiously looked inside before he entered. Five men stood at the bar, two of them obviously so drunk they could hardly remain upright. This pair had their revolvers in hand, weaving slightly while they tried to sight on the glass eye of a stuffed buffalo head, which decorated the balcony railing.

"Th'r you go, Slim. You missed, too. My turn."

"Th' hell I missed, Garvey! Watch me."

"No ya don'! 'S my turn, damn it!"

Billy Ash entered, his Remington cocked and ready. "Hold it, you men!"

The five trail riders gaped toward the young deputy. Slim and Garvey guffawed openly. Another of the five pushed away from the bar, blinking at the lawmen. "Billy? Billy Ash? Is that you?"

"Huh?" Then recognition came. "Owen Casey? I'm right, ain't I?"

"Damn right you're right." Casey was as drunk as his men. "The same Owen Casey who used to whip yer tail every Friday after school back in the fifth grade."

Billy frowned, trying to look stern. "You're making yourself quite notorious around the territory. I don't know that I like having you in our town."

An incredulous look crossed Casey's face, then he laughed heartily. "You lawin' around here now?"

"I am."

Sudden fury darkened Owen Casey's face. "Then get on with your door shakin'. This here's men's doin's. You heard me, git now!"

"These two men are breaking the law, Owen. I intend to take 'em in for it. The police court will set their fines in the morning."

A glint of animal cunning lighted Owen Casey's eye. "You fixin' to take all five of us, Billy? Gonna use that li'l peashooter?"

Billy Ash braced himself, determined not to be bluffed out by a former town bully. "If I have to."

A lopsided, wicked grin spread on Casey's face. From the corner of his eye, Billy noticed blurred, rapid motion and heard the ratcheting clicks of hammers being drawn back. Owen and the other four snickered openly.

"These three are friends of ours, Billy. Ride with us. And it seems you're outgunned. Now back down and leave us to our fun."

As Billy eyed the men at a nearby table, sudden sureness of impending death cooled his ardor for enforcing the law. Eyes wide and heart fluttery, he backed to the bat wings and pushed out onto the boardwalk, hindside first. "I'll be back. If you know what's good for you, you'll all be gone when I get here." Billy turned and started away, stiff legged.

Behind him he heard the raucous laughter of the small-time desperados who had faced him down. Bitter defeat roiled in his stomach. Once clear of the building front, Billy broke into a trot, hurrying toward Clay Rider's distant house. With each footstep that pounded on the dusty street, Billy gulped for breath and angrily fought back the tears of humiliation that gathered to run down his face.

Clay and Howie had heard the gunshots, much muted by distance, and paused in their game. Neither spoke. In a few moments they heard Billy's pounding footsteps. The teen-aged lawman clumped up on the rickety porch and pounded on Clint's door.

"Marshal Rider . . . Marshal Rider!" Billy began yelling even before Clint opened the door. When the portal swung inward, yellow lamplight spilled on the boy's wide-eyed, frightened face. "Owen Casey's in town. He's got a gang of toughs with him. They're shootin' up the Golden Horn. There's eight of them."

"Okay, Billy. You done good in comin' for me. Howie, grab that shotgun."

"I can't help you, Clint. You know I don't approve of violence in enforcing the law. I'd only be in the way."

"Now, dang it, Howie. I need more'n one deputy to face eight armed men. An' Matt Dolan'll be liquored up so much he can't see across a street. All you got to do is point that ten gauge at them while Billy and I disarm the bunch and herd them off to jail. Heck, if they was local boys, all boozed up, you wouldn't even have to load it. As things stand, though," Clint went on, ignoring Howie's agitated, but silent, protests, "you'd best drop in a couple rounds of double-oh. No man's fool enough to stand up to that chopped-off Wells Fargo gun. Not even a hairpin like Owen Casey. Let's go."

Three minutes later, the men waited in position. Clint and Howie would enter the front, through the bat wings of the Golden Horn, while Billy went to the side entrance and slipped quietly in to get Owen Casey and his gang in a crossfire. Billy had taken time to retrieve a Henry repeating rifle from the rack in the marshal's office. Howie fidgeted nervously beside Clint as the broad-shouldered marshal took a deep breath and stepped through the swinging door.

"Everybody freeze!"

Howie moved to Clint's left and raised the twin muzzles of the shotgun until they leveled on the belt buckles of the five men at the bar. Owen Casey, whose drinking had begun to effect his vision, turned slowly, unsteadily, from the rail in front of him, squinting to see clearly.

"Ha? Who th' hell's this?"

"I'm the marshal, and you men are under arrest."

"You're makin' a mistake, marshal. You just go back

to mindin' your own business and we'll mind ourn." Casey's hand, and those of two of his men, sidled toward holstered weapons.

"You heard the marshal! Nobody moves!" Howie's voice slid up the scale from tenor to contralto to soprano, surprising himself more through the mere act of speaking out than he did those he faced. At the round deal table to the left, the three seated gunslingers closed fingers around the butts of their revolvers.

A ratcheting sound at their backs, as Billy chambered a round in the Henry, melted their determination. They sat rigid, eyes taking in the play, hands on the table. A foolish grin spread over Owen Casey's face.

"Howie? Howie Wilkins? A sissy like you's got no call buttin' into this. Go back to countin' yer buttons." He turned his attention to Clint Rider. "What say you tell this store clerk to back off with that scattergun, marshal? Let's settle this man to man. An' if you don't mind, what's your name? I always like to know who it is I'm about to plant."

"Watch the others, Howie."

"But, Clint . . ." Too late. Clint Rider took two purposeful strides toward the bar, his hand dropped to the Remington at his hip.

"My name's Rider, Clint Rider."

Clint took two more steps while Owen's face paled. He knew the name, had heard many times of the reputation and had learned long ago to fear and respect both. His hand, though, streaked toward leather, fingers closing on the butt of his Colt Army .45 and drawing it free from the soft leather pouch holster. Clint drew then, too, though he didn't slip-thumb the hammer.

Instead, he raised his gun to shoulder height and whipped it viciously across in front of him. The heavy barrel connected with the side of Owen's head with a solid clunk. The would-be gunman's eyes crossed, then rolled upward in his head, and he fell solidly to the sawdust-strewn floor.

For a second no one moved. Then Clint turned to the others. "Shuck those irons, boys." They quickly complied.

"Two of you pick up Casey there and bring him along. March!" When Billy Ash began herding the miscreants through the bat wings, Clay turned to Howie, a warm, friendly grin creasing his sun-darkened, weather-gullied face.

"You did fine, Howie. Just fine. I'm proud of you."

Although basking in his friend's approval, Howie could only think of what Amy would say were she to know. He managed a sickly grimace in reply.

Riney Stark leaned back with satisfaction, spreading his cards on the table, revealing a full house. Then he reached out and raked in the pot. "Never buck a pat hand, my daddy used to say. Never buck a pat hand. That's where you boys made your mistake. Now, finish up yer drinks and we hit the trail. We'll make camp on the desert tonight."

The outlaws looked as though they might make further protests. Marv saw this as an opportunity to make points with Riney, so he drew back his chair and started to stand.

"Whatever you say, boss," Marv said agreeably. "Let's

ride." Marv received a kick under the table from Charlie for his efforts.

The gang rose, though, and left the cantina. They swung into their saddles and turned from the tie rail, spurred their horses into a gallop and scattered barefoot children out of the way as they rode down the main street of Nogales into the night-dark desert.

Chapter 4

Natana-jo sat astride his foam-flecked horse, his naked thighs glistening with sweat. Before him, at his mount's neck, stood Satanta, chief scout of *Natana-jo*'s band. The war chief listened gravely while Satanta evaluated the conditions he had discovered in the white-eye camp.

"One night they slept here. The six men who raided our village. See there and there." Satanta pointed to a large ring of blackened sand with an earth-covered mound of coals, still shimmering. "They made a big fire, like men unafraid. They cooked and ate of the stinking meat *Pen-dik-olye* call beef, and buried the remains in the hide. My nose found that for me," he added with a fleeting smile. Several warriors made the grunting sounds that passed for laughter among the Apache, the first sign of levity since discovering the massacre of their village. Satanta continued:

"Early this morning they ride out. The sign shows they still head to *Mejico*."

"You have done well, Satanta. Take your scouts and ride on now. Bring us word of their destination." *Natana-jo* turned to his warriors, his voice rising in pitch as he exhorted them. "Think of our people, dead and mutilated. Think of those we loved and will see no more. Then think on these white-eyes and their friends the *Me-ji-kanos*. When we find the place where these *hijos de putas* sell the scalps of our people, we must harden our hearts. We must become like our brothers, the Mescaleros, and kill them every one: the men, women, and children. We must even kill their burros, cattle, and dogs. I have spoken."

"What of those who did this terrible thing? Are only the *Me-ji-kanos* to be punished?"

Natana-jo looked at the boy and remembered that he had lost his grandfather, little brother, *Honapi Taksin*, and his mother. "Foolish *Tamka*. I have said it before, and this I promise you now. When we find these men they shall be slow in dying. They shall scream for a long time and beg for a bullet to end their suffering for many days before their lives leave their bodies. This will be spoken of no more."

Natana-jo's sober black eyes met the unwavering, blank stare of each of his warriors in turn, sealing his word. When at last all seemed satisfied, he raised his hand, clutching a breech-loading Sharps, his bronze arm stark against the midday sun.

"How many miles you reckon we made today, Riney?"

"Better'n forty, Charlie, by my figures. That leaves us another day's travel to Montenegro, and a hard one at that."

Charlie Bell laid down the armful of fallen branches he'd gathered and rubbed vigorously at his backside.

"Oh, my achin' buns. Sunup to sundown, you figger?"

"And then some allowin' for rests for the critters."

Charlie began building a cook fire while Riney seated himself and leaned back against his saddle, easing the cramped muscles of legs and shoulders. Marv Hoyle came over and hunkered down beside the outlaw leader.

"Is it true you were a major during the war, Riney?"

"Huh? How's that? Oh, sorry, Marv, I was thinkin' about the job ahead of us. You asked about the war?"

"Yes, sir."

"Well, I rode with ol' Brax Bragg's cavalry in the Army of Tennessee. Though I was only a captain. Weren't many majors in either army then. Ain't now, for that matter. We had us a time, though."

"Did you fight in any of the big battles?"

"I did my share, I suppose. The Haymarket . . . Pea Ridge . . ." Riney's voice faltered, and Marv swore he could see water welling up in the outlaw's eyes. "Vicksburg . . . I lost my brother there. I was detached to try find a way through enemy lines to hit 'em in the rear. Ya see, ol' Useless Grant had us bottled up in the town and the bluffs to the northeast. Anyhow, when I was bringin' my boys back, this charge starts right in front of us. I was close enough I could recognize faces. Leadin' 'em was my brother, Sigfried. Our artillery opened up and cut him down at the head of his men."

Marv's eyes went wide. "You mean our artillery was shootin' down our own boys?"

"Naw. It . . . it weren't that way at all. You see, Sig had been to the academy. He had him this commission from the congress an' all and stayed with the Union. He was leadin' a Yankee charge to attack our flank.

First time I ever saw a man get his head took off with a cannonball. I loved my brother more than life itself, even if he was a Yankee. I mourned him a long time after that. There was good times, too, though.

"I recall one time we rode into this Loosiana town. It was during the retreat from Vicksburg. One building, removed a couple of blocks from the square had this fancy front and a big ol' brass plaque beside the door. The engravin' on the thing said it was Miss Leitner's Academy for Refined Young Ladies. Well now, them *refined* young ladies were learnin' some mighty interesting things at *that* school, I'll tell you. Turned out to be the biggest bawdy house in town, packed brim full of lovely chippies. There weren't a one of us that had strength enough to swing up into the saddle the next morning. Ol' Wheeler, our commander, read us the riot act, quoted a lot of high-flown things outta that Bible he always carried, and we was one sore bunch of cavalry that rode outta that place, that I'll guarantee."

"C'n y'all stop that jawin' long enough to eat some grub? It's hot and it's ready," Charlie Bell called our when the laughter of the gang died down.

"That's all you can say for it, with Charlie cookin'," Davey contributed.

"The *rancheria* that the *Me-ji-kanos* call Nogales is one sleep away," Satanta told his chief. His high-top moccasins, leggins and bronze skin were coated with trail dust, and he breathed with deep, rapid intakes of air. "The white-eyes' trail leads directly there."

Natana-jo thought for a moment. "If we do not stop for darkness, we can be at Nogales when the Sky

Father next lights the east. That is good. Come, we ride to Nogales."

Sunrise crept slowly into the small canyon where Riney Stark and his gang camped. The starveling cottonwood trees rattled in a quickening breeze, and the gang's horses drank noisily from a small spring. Charlie and Marv sat near the cook fire, Charlie cutting slices from a slab of bacon. Nearby, his shirt and long johns' top hanging from his waist, Pearly stood with his back crooked at an odd angle. He squinted into a small scrap of mirror, propped in a notch of a tall cholla cactus. With elaborate gestures, he labored to shave himself. At the sight of him, Marv put a self-conscious hand to his smooth cheek and jawline, moving his eyes to look closely at the others.

Everyone but him, he realized with almost guilty disappointment, showed a stubble of beard, the result of two days without barbering. No wonder they think I'm not good for anything but a fetchin' boy, he thought darkly. He might not have a beard, he reckoned keenly, but he could hold his own when the action started. Perk walked to the fire, taking a seat beside Marv and ending the boy's speculations.

Perk added a few finishing touches to a small gallows he had whittled from the soft flesh of a cottonwood. He examined it critically, then tossed it on the blaze. Bending forward he poured himself a cup of coffee.

"Mornin', Charlie, Marv."

"Good mornin', Perk." Marv looked at the lanky outlaw with a sudden birth of hope. Almost pleadingly he asked his question. "I did pretty good the other day, didn't I, Perk?"

"Oh, I suppose so. We all had us some work to do." Perk took a sip of the bitter black brew, winced at the heat that seared his upper lip and sat the cup aside to cool. "How many you figger you got, kid?"

"Oh, at least killed off ten myself. For certain I scalped more'n a dozen."

Charlie Bell could never resist an opportunity to feel superior to someone. "They was them raggedy ones I saw in the bag, eh?"

Wounded pride caused Marv to flare up defensively. " 'Tweren't no such thing! Davey taught me real good how to take a scalp." Still smarting, he sought to change the subject. "Say, Perk, how many men you killed in your life?"

Perk considered the question slowly, a distant look on his face, as though uncertain of a figure so enormous. "Well . . . now . . . not countin' the war . . . near as I can calculate it must be . . . oh, I'd say 'bout forty-eight, forty-nine."

Across the fire Charlie stopped stirring the bacon long enough to take a big bite off his twist of tobacco and chomp on it a moment. Once he'd worked the cud into place he eyed Perk askance. "Come on, now, Perk. You know Injuns and niggers don't count."

Marv, unsure if he was being kidded again or not, turned a puzzled look from one to the other. At Perk's reply, he shrugged off the feeling his leg was being pulled.

"Wall, then . . . must be 'bout an even two dozen. Mezkins *do* count, don't they, Charlie?"

Charlie's lips pursed into a parody of a brown-rimmed kiss, and he elaborately spit a long stream of tobacco juice before answering, his face as solemn and sincere as Perk's.

" 'Course not, Perk. What ever put that in your head?"

Perk appeared crestfallen. "Huh. That bein' the rule, I figger at the most some nine or ten . . . maybe eleven men."

Marv had been definitely impressed by this revelation. The admiring gaze he turned on Perk Perkins clearly revealed that even before he let slip a childish expression of wonder.

"Gol-lee! And . . . and here I thought I'd done somethin' big killin' those six 'Paches." Marv took out his sixgun and put it on half-cock.

He began to idly spin the cylinder with his finger until he recalled with embarrassment the notches he'd so proudly carved in the butt to commemorate the Apache women and children he'd slain. Regretting his foolish deed, he hastily returned the Remington to its soft pouch holster. As he did, Pearly walked over, his shave finished, and he spooned beans onto a tin plate. He helped himself to some bacon and sat, cross-legged, beside Marv. He placed a hand on the boy's shoulder and gave him a reassuring pat. When being earnest, Pearly's Boston accent become most pronounced.

"Don't take that pair seriously, Marv. You did exceedingly well in my book."

"Why . . . thank you, Pearly. Thanks a lot." Marv beamed in the abundance of praise from the handsome outlaw.

Charlie Bell made a sour face and worked the cud of tobacco around in his mouth again before addressing himself to Pearly. "Well, well. If it ain't li'l ol' pretty one hisself. Quiet as you was we figgered you musta done us a favor and cut your throat." To Marv he continued in a nasty tone of voice. "Pretty Boy here, he ain't much for gunfightin'. He's more of a ladies man." He winked broadly at Marv before thrusting his last barb at Pearly.

"Heard tell he mussed up a couple real bad over Texas way once. Am I right, Pearly?" Cackling laughter rolled out of Charlie's tobacco-stained mouth, joined by Davey and Perk.

Pearly threw the contents of his coffee cup at Charlie, who scuttled out of the way in time to avoid the scalding liquid. He shook his finger at Pearly like a parent chiding a child, then stopped abruptly when Riney strode purposefully toward them.

"That's enough outta you rowdies. We ride out soon as we can." Riney turned to Marv. "Marv, you clean up the camp. And do it right this time. We don't want any sign of our bein' here."

Orders putting him back on his seemingly endless, onerous task, coming immediately on top of Pearly's words of praise, put a tone of wounded dignity in Marv's voice. "*Me* clean up? Why do I always have to do it?"

Riney's usually placid features turned hard with sudden anger. "There somethin' wrong with your hearin', boy?"

Marv remained seated and now Riney towered over him. Afraid now of what his defiance had provoked, but equally determined not to back down in front of the others, Marv plunged on. "Riney, I've been doin' nothin' but the scut work since I joined up. Leadin' horses, cleanin' up and the like ain't my idea of what outlawin's all about." Marv shoved to his feet, fisted hands on his hips. The others could see it took a conscious effort for the youngster to carry on his rebellion.

"I did my share of killin' in that Apache village. Figure I ain't a beginner anymore. I'm as good as anyone in this outfit. That means we take turns. Have Charlie do it." Marv spun on one heel and started to walk away.

Riney's anger overcame him. With a single step he closed the distance between them. One muscular arm lashed out and grabbed Marv by the shoulder. Riney whirled Marv around and backhanded him, staggering the slightly built boy. "I'm bossin' this outfit, damn you boy, and I give the orders. For the last time, *clean up this camp!*"

Marv took a couple of stumbling steps backward, then squared off to face Riney. His right hand lightly caressed the butt of his Remington. Riney shifted his weight and braced for a shootout. He didn't want to kill this kid. He needed an extra gun for the silver holdup. He'd do it if he had to, though. It depended on what Marv chose to do from here. Riney relaxed when Marv pushed the fight with his mouth.

"I said I was as good as anybody here. You have someone else clean up." Desperation had begun to glaze Marv's eyes.

"Maybe you reckon you're as good as me? Figger you can take me?" Riney's hand poised over his own revolver.

In that instant Marv realized his rash words had gotten him in too deep. Hastily he tried to mend a badly shattered fence. "Well, now, I . . . I never said that, Riney. That is . . . I . . ." Unbidden, Marv's perverse resentment rose again, choking off his words of conciliation. "But if it ever came to that, I suppose I could . . . ha, ha, bein', uh, younger and all."

"Well, you got to, boy. Right now!"

Marv blanched white and sent a trembling left hand flashing to his belt buckle to release it and let his gun harness fall to the ground. Riney crossed the short distance between them in two quick strides. His hard-knuckled fist snapped out and caught Marv under the left cheekbone.

Marv stumbled back, off balance, his arms windmilling. Riney moved in relentlessly, driving powerful lefts and rights to Marv's rib cage. Finally the boy recovered enough to block one of Riney's blows and snap a short left jab that glanced off Riney's shoulder. Undeterred, Riney came in again, punching Marv in the midsection, doubling him with sledgehammer strokes to the bread basket. A looping right to the side of Marv's head straightened him up. Only his fierce determination to make a good showing in front of the rest of the gang kept him on his feet. Marv backpeddled furiously and managed to bring up his guard.

It did him little good. Shoulders rolling with each swing, Riney waded in again. Marv absorbed a fearsome amount of punishment. He even managed to catch Riney with a stinging blow on one ear and follow up with a left-right combination that snapped back the gang leader's head. Then seemingly out of nowhere, Riney's fist connected with the hinge of Marv's jaw, the middle knuckle mashing into the bundle of nerves there. The world spun and grew black while Marv's head rang and buzzed, then his vision cleared.

Marv found himself down on one knee, without any recollection of how he got there. His head hung low, and blood dripped from his nose and mouth. He looked up in time to see the pointed toe of Riney's boot rushing at his exposed face. Marv dodged to the side quickly enough to take the kick on his shoulder. The force knocked him backward, into the air, to sprawl in the dirt, all fight taken from him. Still Riney didn't stop.

He closed in and drove a vicious heel stomp to Marv's groin, barely missing bladder, testicles, and penis as the boy twisted violently to one side, taking the blow near the point of one hip. Marv screamed at the pain and continued to cry out while Riney kicked him in the ribs and thighs. At last, his fury spent, Riney bent down and grabbed a handful of Marv's frilly shirt front. He dragged the youth partway upright, giving him a shake for good measure.

"You through tryin' to boss my gang? Got any more orders you want to give to me? Now then. If it weren't we needed an extra hand on this robbery, I'd have gunned you down on the spot. Might have done so even then if your mouth didn't show me you hadn't the guts to pull an iron on me. If you want to ride with this gang from now on, you take your orders like everyone else and you see they're carried out no matter what. Is that clear?"

"Y-yes, sir. Sure, Riney."

Riney Stark stood erect and brushed the crumbs of sand from his trouser knees. He turned to the others. "Saddle up, boys. We got a lot of ridin' to do. An', Davey," Riney said and pointed toward the beaten Marv, "scoop up that trash and pour it on a horse, will you?"

Charlie Bell started toward the spring with a collapsible leather water pale. "You have to go and pound him that hard, Riney?" he grumbled. "Least you coulda done was wait until he had this place cleaned up. Now I gotta do it."

Chapter 5

Cholla, ocatillo, and lonely pipe organ cactus sparsely dotted the rolling sand hills outside Montenegro in the blazing heart of the Chihuahua desert. Here and there a valiant smoke tree lifted lacy leaves to the sky, struggling to survive the inferno, which burned down at mid-morning. Six riders, in a ragged, irregular line, appeared out of the shimmering heat waves, their horses plodding slowly, like hobbled snails, their heads down with exhaustion and thirst. At a rusty, croaking shout from the man in the lead, the others came out of their lethargy and reined their mounts in the direction he pointed.

The animals sensed the presence of water nearby and flared delicate nostrils, then increased the pace. With the eager yells of men near their absolute limit, the Riney Stark gang kicked even greater speed out of their steeds, angling down the face of a steep sloping hill toward a cluster of fragile willow trees which nestled around a fresh water spring.

"Right where the Comanche war legends say it would be," Davey exulted when he and the others dismounted and led their horses to the water's edge. Cautiously, at first, they let the beasts take a few swallows, forcibly pulled them back and drank themselves before allowing the animals more. When all had drunk their fill, Riney signed to Charlie that he wanted to talk to him alone. The two men walked away from the others, found a spot under a large, ancient willow and took seats there. Davey and Marv staked out the tired critters to graze on what grass remained at the small oasis. While they did so, Riney silently studied Charlie, wondering how to impress on the man's limited wit the importance of the mission he was to be assigned. At last he spoke in an earnest tone:

"Charlie, I want you to ride into Montenegro and find out all you can about that silver shipment. We need to know if the train will come through tomorrow afternoon like planned, how many guards on it and if they figure to stay overnight in town or go on."

Charlie frowned. "And I suppose I just go up to somebody in town and ask them all those questions? How am I gonna find out all that? I can't speak that Mezkin lingo."

"There's enough Americans in town. You can talk to them without arousing suspicion. You know how to do it. Say, when the wagon train rolls into town, you can remark to some American on the street that it sure looks like something important with all those soldiers along . . . something like that."

"Yeah, yeah, sure, Riney. I got you now."

"The thing is you've got to use your head, Charlie."

"Like I can see iffin they's rooms open in the hotel for tomorrie night, 'cause those fancy Mezkins allies stays there. How's that Riney? How's that for usin' my head?"

"That's good, Charlie. Now, you stay in town all afternoon and evening." Riney paused and then added more force to his words. "And you keep outta trouble, Charlie, ya hear? Next thing. If they don't stay over, get on your horse and hightail it out to the canyon."

Charlie replied with almost childlike eagerness. "I know the rest, Riney. Really I do. You an' the boys'll have the dynamite set in the canyon. We wait for the *federales* and then . . . *blooie*! The silver is ours. I can sure outrun those heavy wagons on that critter o' mine and be there to let you know. That's a smart plan, Riney. I'm sure glad you're boss."

Riney rose to his feet and began to walk slowly back to the others. His mind, as always, wondered if tribute from Charlie Bell wasn't a dubious honor.

Perk had a small fire going, coffee bubbling in a pot. Davey, who had disappeared from camp for a while, returned with three plump rabbits. He quickly skinned and gutted them and hung them on willow branches over the fire.

"Fresh meat for a change," he commented, flashing a bright smile at Riney.

"Good idea. Now gather around boys. We're going over this again. We'll take it from where the dynamite goes off.

"Charlie will be back with us by then. He and you, Pearly, ride down the left bank to the wagons. Don't start to fire until you're close enough not to miss a single shot."

"Right. Most of the time the dust will hide us as we ride down."

"You've got it, Pearly. Perk, you and Davey here will come down from the other side, then Marv and I close the trap from front and rear."

"How do we keep from shootin' each other?" Marv hazarded.

"You don't shoot at anyone that isn't directly in front of you and no further away than a few feet. Those Mezkin *federales* will be in their brown trail outfits or else in their fancy green and red uniforms. No problem telling them from us. After the first shock wears off they'll be shootin' back, but don't let that worry you."

"Yeah. They're gonna figure we got twenty, thirty boys with us when we all cut loose." To Marv's puzzled look, Davey went on to explain. "Lots of echoes in that canyon. We'll be blastin' away from above them. Once those *federales* begin shootin', too, they won't be able to tell how many they're facin'."

"All of which is to our advantage. Any more questions?"

"Yeah, Riney. What happens if they got more guards than we can handle?"

"That's why I'm sending Charlie into town, Perk. If he sees too many riders with the wagons, he can tell us and we can try pickin' off a few at a time and leadin' them on a goose chase until the rest get into the canyon."

"Won't that warn them so they'll be ready for us?" Marv asked.

"They will know that *something* is going to happen, but they won't know what or where. That dynamite is the same as our artillery. Those *federales* won't be expecting a few long riders taking potshots at them to come on like an army. It's part of our element of surprise, Marv, and knowin' we're out there won't help 'em a bit when it comes to that."

Perk spat a long stream of tobacco juice into the gray-white ash at the edge of the fire. "If that don't work, do we just forget the whole thing?"

"Probably have to," Riney said regretfully.

Charlie Bell seemed to see his longed-for wealth flying out of his reach. A slight tic developed below his left eye, a danger signal Riney Stark had long been familiar with. "They better not have too many guards. I . . . I'll gun 'em all down in town if they do."

Riney turned on Charlie, an angry glare on his face. For a moment, the chubby outlaw looked back blankly, then revised his features into an ingratiating expression, flashing his boss a weak smile. From experience, Riney ignored it.

"I'm warnin' you again, Charlie. You better take care not to get in any kind of trouble in town. Is that clear?"

Charlie correctly read the craggy countenance and icy gaze of his leader, and words spilled nervously from him. "I . . . I was only funnin', boss. Just funnin'."

"Your idea of funnin' is going to get you killed one of these days, Charlie. When you get to Montenegro, you look around and listen good and remember what you see and hear. And nothin' else, hear?"

"Sure, sure, Riney. You want I should leave right now?"

Charlie rose expectantly and began to walk toward his hobbled horse, glad to get away from Riney's angry glare. He gained back his confidence with each stride when no further admonitions or instructions followed him. Behind Charlie, Pearly leaned forward and poked a stick into the dying fire. He cast a baleful glance in Charlie's direction and sighed heavily.

"I sure hope nothin' goes wrong, sendin' *him* into town."

The hot morning sun that had illuminated Riney Stark's camp shined equally on Nogales, Sonora, Mexico. Its rays fought a battle with several orange flickering fires, which burned brightly in the charred hulks of what had once been homes and business establishments. Several resolute defenders still held out in the church on the main plaza, but their priest could no longer give them moral support. The padre had been impaled on an Apache war lance that fastened him to the outside of one thick wooden panel of the tall double doors. From the angle of an intersecting street, *Natana-jo* directed a group of warriors.

"They cannot last long. When there is no longer feed for their guns, burn them out or let them die in the fire of their meeting lodge." The squat, muscular pug-faced Apache received the acknowledgements of his men and turned his pony to ride in the direction of the small military compound. Along his route, the street was littered with the bodies of men, women, and children, unfortunates who had not been able to escape the Apache dawn attack. Long before he reached the high dun walls, he heard the rhythmic screaming from inside.

Natana-jo reined up and impassively studied the fat soldier lying slumped over the parapet, his chest decorated with Apache arrows. The Mexican's lips were drawn back in the rictus of death, and his teeth still tightly clamped the cold stub of a cigar. *Natana-jo* nodded in satisfaction and rode through the open gates.

Corpses of soldiers littered the ground in a tight ring where the garrison made its final stand. Across the inner courtyard the Mexican soldiers had previously dug a large barbecue pit for festive occasions when they would roast half a beef at a time. It now served a far grimmer purpose. From here came the solitary, ululating scream, ceaseless and agonizing.

The *commandante* hung by his heels, suspended head down over a small, low fire carefully constructed so it wouldn't burn too hot and quickly kill him, but rather slowly roast his brain and boil the blood gathered inside his skull until it exploded. He had been stripped of his fancy red and green uniform jacket with its gold braid and glittering medals and his lace-fronted white shirt. His hands were secured behind his back and far from the tiny flicker of flame so that he could do nothing to hasten a merciful death. *Natana-jo* rode close by to observe.

"He is the last to die," an old warrior informed his chief. "The *jefe de soldados*. Most fitting."

Natana-jo's teeth flashed white in a brief grin of contentment. "Make sure it takes a long while." Then he switched to Spanish so the tortured man could understand. "These Mexicans, at least, will buy no more Apache scalps."

Chapter 6

Montenegro lay in a broad, fertile valley between the sere desert plateau of the Chihuahua desert and the verdant foothills of the Sierra Madre Occidental. A placid river meandered through the wide, well-tended fields and bent around the eastern edge of the city. It twinkled invitingly to Charlie Bell when he topped the final rise, and he stared downslope to the sleepy-looking town.

Charlie urged his mount into a trot when a loud rumble rose complainingly from his distended belly, emphasizing how hungry he really felt. Few people stirred in the late afternoon sun; mostly farmers, working their fields in a meticulously slow manner. As a result, Charlie's passage went relatively unremarked.

When Charlie neared the first buildings, low, pole and sod-roofed adobes, unadorned save for their brightly painted doors, he reined in and tipped back the brim of his hat. Cruel, pig eyes swept the street ahead and the houses for any possible danger. Another grumbling roll from Charlie's innards reminded him of how much he wanted a meal. He touched spurs to his animal's flanks and started down toward the center of

Montenegro.

He soon reached the first well-tended dwellings, their mud-block walls whitewashed, low adobe fences separating the yards from the street. Beyond them came a plethora of similar houses, their front faces done in a kaleidoscope of colors: turquoise, orange, yellow, and blue. Their sidewalls were whitewashed, though a few remained unpainted. Several men, arousing from their siestas, looked incuriously at the gringo who rode past, and Charlie, in turn, nodded curtly to those who managed to make eye contact. Three blocks along he reached the central square.

Montenegro's plaza predated even the Spanish conquest of Mexico. The Meztecs, a vassal state of the Aztec empire, made this area their winter capital. Where the cathedral now dominated one side of the square, a short, flat-topped pyramid once stood, its stone alter stained with the blood of many sacrifices. The large, tree-packed park at the center had once been the barren, hard-pounded native marketplace. The Spaniards had wrought their usual changes and, when they had gained independence from the mother country, the Mexicans had effected more.

The municipal buildings, the police station, and jail fronted one side of the plaza. A large, elegant hotel, several fine restaurants, and prosperous business establishments formed the third side. Along the fourth face, saloons, eateries, small shops, and second class, walk-up hotels vied for customers. Charlie Bell turned his horse along this latter block. He reined up in front of an establishment that advertised both food and drink. Charlie's mouth watered in anticipation as he swung out of the saddle.

Charlie slip-reined his horse over the hitch rail and started toward the boardwalk, wondering how he could accomplish what Riney had sent him to do. He understood little Spanish and spoke even less. Among the words he considered important to know he counted *comidas* (meals or food) to be the primary one; the others being; cantina (saloon), *cerveza* (beer), *puta* (whore), and tequilla. Charlie's foot had only landed on the walkway when a small, ragtag boy accosted him.

The youngster, who had scurried over from the park, wore a patched, faded serape over well-worn, pajama-like white shirt and trousers. He was barefoot and clutched a battered straw sombrero in his hands. He appeared to be in that indeterminate age, somewhere between eight and eleven. His dark eyes looked up at Charlie in open appeal.

"Buenas tardes, señor."

Charlie looked down at the youngster, and a slow, simple smile creased his lips. From his vest pocket he withdrew a peso coin. "Why, howdy, boy."

The child ducked his eyes, one hand extended for the money, mumbling in Spanish as though ashamed of begging. "The *señor* is most gracious. My family is so poor, and we have a great need of money."

Uncomprehending, Charlie continued in slowly drawled English. "You want to make a peso, boy?"

Unable to understand the foreign tongue, mistaking Charlie's gesture for charity, the boy took the peso and made it disappear under his serape. Meanwhile, Charlie continued to explain his wants.

"You take my horse down to the stable, have him grained an' watered an' rubbed down real good. You understand me?"

"Gracias, senñor." The boy turned and started to retreat, without taking Charlie's horse. Charlie's eyes flew open in surprise. His slow brain tried to digest this situation while he reached out automatically to grab the youngster by the shoulder and jerk him back.

"Where you goin', boy? I tole you to take my *caballo* down to the livery! Your gonna do it or give me that 'dobe dollar, ya hear?"

The boy, frightened by the angry tone of the foreign words, cringed in front of Charlie while tears filled his eyes. He begged understanding in his high-pitched voice.

"Espere me, señor! No comprendo ingles."

For a moment, Charlie saw himself in the youngster's place, standing in his yard at home, sobbing while the evil men with the badges and shotguns had blown off his father's head. The memory summoned, as always, a white-hot, insane rage. Charlie's hand flashed out. The thick, muscular fingers entwined in the child's hair, jerked him off his feet and shoved the boy roughly against the tie rail. A wild glow of madness burned in Charlie's eyes as he began to shake the lad.

"Y'er like all the rest, takin', always takin'. Boy, I don't understand that gabble talk o' yourn, but I'll tell you this. When I say for you to do somethin', you, by God, do it, ya hear?"

The boy cried out in anguish, his words distorted by the flailing of his body. *"S-socoro! Socoro, Papi! Por favor, acabarse, señor!"*

Across the street, in the park, a shabbily dressed man, somewhat broken with hard toil and age, came to his feet from under a tree where he had been dozing and started toward the altercation. He raised a hand and called out to Charlie.

"Stop it, *señor*, please stop. He is but a little boy."

Charlie ignored the boy's father and continued shaking the lad. He giggled wildly at the pain-glazed eyes of the youngster. Overcome by seeing his son treated in this manner, the man rushed to Charlie and jerked at his left arm.

"I beg you, stop it!" he cried.

For the first time, Charlie noticed the father. Like a sleeper coming out of a deep dream, Charlie slowly turned his head and focused his eyes on the Mexican at his side. The terrifying scene from the past faded, vanished. A look of comprehension crossed Charlie's face, then his features went blank again.

He lashed out with his left arm, backhanded the frail man and sent him reeling out into the street. Although Charlie, in the frenzy of his blood lust, remained totally unaware of it, a crowd had begun to gather, attracted by the disturbance. Angry mutters rose, and shouts of encouragement reached the father's ears.

He bent and picked up a rock, hefted it for weight and throwability. At the same moment, Charlie dropped the boy. The child sank to the ground with a pitiful moan while Charlie spun on the old man, his hand flying to his holster.

Charlie Bell drew with baffling speed, then took time to slowly aim at his target. Undaunted and enraged at the treatment of his son, the Mexican beggar advanced menacingly. Charlie rested the butt of his Remington Model '60 Army on the palm of his left hand, eared back the hammer and squinted along the long notch of the rear sight. When the father of the injured boy raised his arm to throw his missile, Charlie fired.

His first shot failed to discharge. Quickly he thumbed the hammer and again took aim. The father, seeing death so near, drained of his momentary courageous anger. He dropped the rock and began to back away. Charlie's trigger finger twitched a second time.

The hammer fell, the gun discharged with a crash and a thick, greasy-gray plume of powder smoke blossomed from the muzzle. Through its obscuring billows, Charlie peered intently, a lop-sided grin on his face, and chortled gleefully at the sight of his victim.

The scrawny old man, struck in the stomach, turned halfway around and his knees buckled. He fell to the ground, emitting a sighing grunt. Behind Charlie, the Mexican boy screamed in terror at the sight of his father shot down in such a manner. Charlie ignored the child and addressed himself to the dying man in front of him.

"You stay the hell outta my business, greaser!" Charlie reholstered his weapon and turned, his attention drawn by the boy's hysterical sobs. He reached down and drew the lad up by his hair again. One hand groped under the serape for the peso he had given the child. His voice quavered with the wild malice of unthrottled rage.

"I ain't finished with you yet, boy. Where'd you hide that dollar?"

The boy's sobs turned to a frightened whimper.

Charlie snorted with disgust and stood erect, seeing the crowd for the first time. "Any of you greasers understand me enough to tell this boy to gimme back the peso he took from me?"

Outside of angry growls, they paid him no attention,

so Charlie went back to slamming the boy's head against the rail. A surge in the crowd failed to attract him. Even the approving murmurs of the people did not deter his actions until the twin barrels of a ten-gauge shotgun rammed against the back of Charlie's neck.

An oily fear sweat broke out on Charlie's forehead, and his eyes bugged with a private terror all his own. A facial tic tugged at the right corner of his mouth, and his hands trembled. The icy voice of the chief of police only made his horror all the greater.

"*Los manos arriba, cabrón!* I say, poot up your han's, gringo bastard."

Charlie hastened to comply, his bowels turning to water, knees rubbery. Now that he was obviously caught and harmless, several persons in the crowd hurriedly explained, one over the other's voice, what happened. The chief, a thin, spare man with whipcord muscles and a drooping wisp of moustache, reached out while listening, and took Charlie's gun. One man, dressed in the clothes of a vaquero, swung a rope menacingly close to Charlie's face. Charlie blanched even more at sight of this and tried to turn. He got jabbed with the shotgun for his efforts, instantly freezing him in place.

"*Silencio, acallerse!*" The crowd obediently quieted. "Now, *señor* butcher, we will find out what happened here." The *jefe* turned to the frightened, bleeding boy. "Panchito, *que passe aqui?*"

The boy wiped his tears of grief and pain and answered. "*Señor jefe*, this man rode into town. I . . . as you know, my family is poor and . . . he looked so rich. I came to ask for money for food. He does not speak our language, but he understood and gave me a peso. I thanked him and started to go when he grabbed me and began to beat my head against the tie rail. I called for help and . . . and my father came." Tears began to flow down Panchito's face again, bitter emotion choking his words. "He . . . this one . . . the gringo . . . he shot my father when he tried to help me." Shaken beyond further endurance, Panchito turned away and buried his face in the ample skirts of a woman nearby. She unfolded him in her arms and let him sob uncontrollably. The crowd muttered angrily again, and the vaquero shook his rope, slapping Charlie's face a number of times. Charlie wilted in the presence of this hostility and, when the pressure of the shotgun relaxed slightly, he turned to face the *jefe*. His voice echoed his abject fear.

"Y-you . . . you, uh, ain't gonna let 'em do anything to me, are you?"

"No, *señor* butcher. I am the *jefe* — the chief of police. They will do nothing to you . . . yet. Tomorrow, when the *federales* arrive, we will have your trial. The day after that . . . we shall hang you, gringo *cabrón*."

A few embers still glowed like red-orange eyes in the deep night that filled *Cañon Diablo*, though the sun rose steadily on the distant horizon. Three of the gang sat around the fire, shovels at their sides, sipping rapidly cooling cups of coffee. They had worked by moonlight, planting dynamite charges in the loose shale sides along the steeply sloping walls of Devil's Canyon. After a breakfast of fatback and beans they would complete their task in daylight. Riney Stark joined his men and poured a cup of the strong, gritty brew. He paused with the cup partway to his mouth at the sound of rattling stones.

Davey Two-Knife slithered down the last of the shale bank and walked to the fire. He held a large, expensive pair of field glasses in one hand. His face wore a grim expression.

"Any sign of him yet?"

"Not a thing, Riney. It's broad daylight over the desert floor. From up there I can see all the way to that range of hills outside town. Not even a coyote stirrin' out on the flats."

"Damn it!" the gang leader exploded. "Charlie knows enough to have been back here by sunup. Even if they hadn't pulled into town he should have reported in. Somethin' gone wrong." Riney strode away from the fire a moment, whirled and returned, his decision made. "Marv, you ride on in to Montenegro. Find out what happened."

Marv Hoyle rose from the ground in a smooth, swift movement. His face glowed with expectation and an inner warmth generated by this sudden change of circumstances that placed Riney's trust in him like he'd always wanted.

"Sure thing, Riney. I'll leave right now."

"And, Marv . . . be careful. Whatever that dumb ox has got himself into, you don't want to be connected to him."

Marv looked a little chagrined. Riney didn't need to lecture him like some green kid. Even so, he swallowed his injured pride, excited by this chance to prove himself. "Yes, sir. I'll do what you say."

After Marv had ridden out, the men went about

fixing their morning meal. The sun crept slowly over the canyon rim to shed misty orange light on the far wall. Riney sent Davey back to his lookout spot on the top of the eroded butte that formed one side of the deep cut in the earth and the others to planting charges. Riney rode out to the desert floor and cut some branches of manzanita, which he tied to a long rope to drag behind his horse. It would be a crude, but effective, means to wipe out their tracks and leave the area looking free of human occupancy. The hours wore by with everyone at their assigned tasks. Riney had made his third sweep with the improvised brush when Davey slithered down from his perch.

"Rider comin' this way, Riney," Davey yelled and waved his arm to attract his boss's attention.

Riney wheeled his horse and trotted to Davey's side. "Only one?"

"Yeah. It looks like Marv. And I know. I don't like it any more'n you."

Ten minutes later Marv Hoyle reined his lathered mount to a dust-clouded halt beside Riney and Davey. His face glistened with sweat and his shirt had become sodden from perspiration. He panted slightly, voice croaking with the dryness of great thirst.

"There's trouble, all right, Riney. Big trouble. They're gonna hang Charlie. Hang him tomorrow."

Davey handed Marv a canteen, and he gulped greedily before completing his report.

"Seems Charlie gunned down some Mezkin. Folks were all set to lynch him but the *jefe* stepped in and took Charlie off to jail. That was yesterday. Couldn't have been in town more'n ten minutes," he added reluctantly.

"Damn that dummy!" Riney cursed with feeling.

"They're gonna have the trial today and, from what I heard, hang him at sunrise tomorrow." Marv drank again.

"Just like that? There has to be more to it, Marv."

"Well . . . uh . . . yeah. Charlie rode into town, the way these greasers tell it, no more'n got there and he starts to beat up on some li'l tadpole kid that done him out of a peso. When the brat's pappy tried to mix in, Charlie shot him." Anticipating Riney's question, Marv reluctantly went on. "The old man didn't have a gun, Riney."

Riney Stark groaned in exasperation. "I never let on I was a feller didn't make mistakes. But I reckon the biggest one I've ever made was sendin' Charlie Bell anywhere without a keeper. What about the silver?"

"No sign of them in town, and they hadn't showed up when I rode out, Riney."

"Just like them Mezkins," Perk interposed. "Mañana will always do. What are you gonna do now, boss?"

Riney studied the faces of his men a long moment. "Well, boys, I don't see we have much choice. We gotta ride in there and get Charlie out. An' all before those soldier boys show up with the silver shipment. Perk, you bring along some of that powder you been plantin' just in case. Saddle up and let's all hit the road."

Chapter 7

Howie Wilkins sat at the kitchen table in their small house two blocks from Colby's main street, letting a cup of coffee grow cold beside his right hand. A medium-sized, metal-strap-bound chest of rich, red cedar lay open before him. Although totally familiar with each item of its contents, Howie's attention remained intently upon each one as he removed it from the box.

First, tied in a faded blue ribbon, came a dozen stock certificates, representing two hundred fifty shares in a worthless gold mine. Howie's father had purchased them during his prosperous days as sheriff. Then, a few years later, the vein had played out. In the interim, Howie's mother had died. His grieving father tried to raise Howie as best he could, being gone frequently to the circuit court to testify or to transport prisoners to jail or a hanging. As a result, he neglected both the boy and his personal affairs. Not until after his death did Howie discover that the stock was worthless. Howie sighed heavily and set the valueless papers aside. He sighed again and reached, somewhat reluctantly, for the next item.

His father's gun: the work-worn, well-cared for sixgun with which Mason Wilkins had tamed a large portion of New Mexico Territory and went on to carry with distinction as a U.S. marshal. A chill of revulsion coursed down Howie's spine when he remembered his mother's words:

"Guns kill people, Howie dear. That's all they are made for. They are things of evil and can do only evil in this world." Her opinion, like Amy's, so differed from his father's and everything in his father's world. Long after she had been laid to rest, the conflicting emotions generated by their opposing viewpoints warred in Howie's mind. Not until he had departed for the East and four years at Yale had he clearly seen matters in the same light as those unaccustomed to the frontier. Yet the lessons of his father's world, often taught with a boxing of his ears or the razor strap, kept returning to him in disquieting real situations, which left him with a sense of helplessness, of somehow being unmanly.

Like that fight in the saloon a few nights before. If Clint hadn't virtually forced him into going, he would never have become involved. Although she constantly nagged at him to be more assertive, dominant, Amy hated violence in any form. So did he. And, likewise, so had his mother.

Yet, throughout his growing years, Howie had seen and heard about his father's using his sixgun and big, hard fists on the side of decency and justice. How, then, could something be both good and evil at the same time? His mother's statement that an inanimate object, a gun, could have a human's will and volition to do anything was idiotic and never entered his mind. She was, after all, his mother. A full year with his philosophy professor, exploring the intricacies of the science of logic, had failed to explain the apparent contradiction; it was vogue in the East to express such silly sentiments as his mother's. Still, one point of view had to be right—the other wrong. At thirty-four, Howie Wilkins had yet to learn which was which. He sat the sixgun aside and reached into the chest once more.

A wide leather belt, cartridge loops sewn on to it, and a semirigid pouch holster attached, came next. It had seen lots of use, and the rich cowhide grain glowed with a deep luster. Pinned through the buckle was a large, shiny silver star, with a bust of blind Justice holding her scale fixed in the center. In arcs above and below were the words, "Sheriff. Freemont County, N. Mex. Territory." Beneath this lay his father's journals, meticulously kept with a list of all expenses and each day's activities when out with a posse, on a lone trail after an outlaw or other law business. Howie knew them by heart. He reached for his cup and winced at the bitter taste of cold coffee. He padded to the sink on slippered feet and dumped the contents down the drain. He took the pot from the stove and refilled the crockery mug. A third time, Howard Wilkins sighed heavily.

He would have to dress for work soon and go down to open the store. Amy hadn't been feeling well, complained of the sniffles, but had promised to join him at noon, bringing him his dinner in a pail. Somehow the thought of having the sole responsibility for the mercantile, if only for half a day, excited him. It made him a bit apprehensive, too. He carried those thoughts down the hall with him as he sipped his coffee.

In the small dressing room off their bedroom, Howie slipped out of his theadbare robe and slid his suspenders off his shoulders. He ladled warm water into the stoneware basin and made ready to shave. Silently he offered up a small prayer that Colby would be spared further violence and discord.

The Riney Stark gang reached Montenegro a little past ten o'clock that morning. They rode in silence, grim faced and determined looking. In the distance a lone church bell tolled mournfully. At the second intersection on a slow-moving procession forced them to halt.

At the head of the funeral cortege came the priest who served the poorer residents of Montenegro from the small chapel where the bell tolled. Behind him walked four acolytes, young Mexican boys bearing a huge crucifix, the banner of the Roman church, and two incense burners. Next came a plain wooden coffin, borne on the work-sloped shoulders of eight peons, its top covered by a scanty blanket of scraggly flowers. Back of it walked the widow, a young, still shapely *señora*, garbed in black and weeping into a small square of handkerchief. She was supported on one side by an aged crone, likewise swathed in a stygian dress. Around them flocked half a dozen children, one whose head was swathed in white bandages, all wailing their grief over their father's passing. Lastly came the official mourners, the friends and neighbors of the deceased. When they spotted the tough, sinister-looking gringos, the procession halted.

Hatred, black as her widow's weeds, flashed from the attractive young woman's obsidian eyes. Here were more evil-looking gringos, like the one who had murdered her Jose. Pearly, always the ladies' man, took in the appealing figure and heart-shaped face, twirled his moustache and flashed a white smile.

"Hey there, pretty one, now that you're foot loose and fancy free, what say we get together at the cantina tonight?"

A look of incomprehension passed over the bereft woman's face. She turned to the old lady beside her. *"Que decir el?"*

"He says . . . this gringo with the filthy mind and the manners of a goat . . . that you should now give yourself to him in the cantina tonight. *Madre de Dios*, such an animal should not be permitted to live." The old woman spat into the dust at the front hoofs of Pearly's horse.

Pearly ignored the exchange and winked broadly. "How about it, honey? We can make us a little whoopee tonight."

"What is the meaning of this?" The priest, shocked, angered, yet a little fearful, waddled up on pudgy legs, his fat body quivering with indignation.

"Just tryin' to console the poor widow, *padre*, by offerin' her a little of what it is makes the world go round." The others in the gang guffawed at Pearly's witticism.

Scarlet suffused the priest's face. "Sacrilege!" he cried in poor, heavily accented English. "I demand you apologize to this poor woman." His nervousness increased when he eyed the collection of arms and the grim faces of the gang.

"You do that iffin you want, *padre*," Perk drawled from his place beside Pearly. "As fer us, we frankly don't give a damn."

Still not able to understand the words in English, the widow turned to the priest, appealing to him for some explanation. "Who are these cruel men, *padre*?"

"Don't fret yourself none, sweety. I'll treat you real nice. Nothin' like a good roll in the hay to take your mind off sad things, I always say."

Perk turned in his saddle, asking over his shoulder, "What she say, Davey?"

Before Davey could answer, the priest interrupted, his voice cold with disdain. "She asked me what type of animals could be so disrespectful of her grief." Before he had finished speaking, Perk and Pearly jumped their mounts forward, hemming in the little priest. Their hands rested menacingly on the butts of their sixguns.

"Watch your tongue, *padre*," Pearly growled. "Them skirts just might not keep us from gunnin' you down."

An angry murmur rose among the men in the procession, though they shrank back from the threat of so many weapons. It took a moment for the priest to recover his composure, but when he did, he replied with venom:

"You are worse than animals. You are demons who walk like men. Where do you come from . . . hell?"

A sudden grin quirked Perk's thin lips. He let his eyes rove insolently over the widow, then the priest. Then he worked his mouth into a sneer, his words sounding ominous:

"You picked as good a place as any, *padre*. That's us, all right. Five devils . . . straight outta hell." He laughed with a wild, hollow sound as the priest's eyes widened, and he crossed himself. Then Perk snarled. "Now get this corpse outta here and bury it before it starts to stink and offends us even more'n you."

At an agitated sign from the priest, the procession moved on, the cleric bending his head close to the widow, talking earnestly to her and casting occasional glances back at the five outlaws sitting in the intersection.

Pearly pushed back the brim of his Stetson and cast a look of feigned innocence at Riney, who sat astride his horse frowning his disapproval of their byplay. Before the gang leader could speak his thoughts, Perk whistled tunelessly.

"Well, I'll be doggone. Flighty bunch, ain't they? Now what say we finds Charlie." He started to rein his horse around to face the main street again when Riney spoke up:

"Just hold on a minute. We *know* where Charlie is. What we gotta learn is how good the law is in this town and what is the best way to go about springin' Charlie outta that *carcel* down there."

Nods of agreement passed among the others. With Riney taking the lead, they all stretched their mounts out to a slow lope, which brought them quickly to the line of smaller saloons, extending off the main plaza. There they reined in at the tie rail and dismounted. They had only stepped up into the boardwalk when the rattle and jingle of fancy harness fittings came to their ears. As one they looked up to see a long column of uniformed *federales* trotting out of the square and bearing down on them. In the van came several heavy-laden wagons.

"Be damned. There goes our silver," Perk murmured in a low voice.

"Right you are," Riney acknowledged. "Couldn't happened at a worse time. Marv. You hang loose out here until they're well outta town. Then trail 'em. If it looks like they're gonna make the canyon before nightfall, hightail it back here. We'll have to hit them and let Charlie go."

Perk shook his head as though he couldn't believe what he had heard. "Do you mean that, Riney? Really mean it? You'd let the greasers hang good ol' Charlie?"

"When it comes to a choice between Charlie Bell and that silver, do we have an alternative?" Riney turned from the others and entered the cool interior of the cantina, knocking dust from his clothes. After a brief exchange of looks among them, in which they all saw grudging agreement with their boss, the gang followed, leaving Merv to keep an eye on the silver train.

Inside the saloon the gang members lined the bar. Davey ordered beer for them all in precise, rapid Spanish. The bartender pulled a long, sad face and informed them that the establishment's barrel was empty and that they had no beer. Davey requested tequilla. The *cantinero* sized up his rough-looking customers and bent below the back bar, rummaging among the bottles ranked there until he came up with one particular container, encased in a basket of woven cactus fiber and covered with dust.

The barkeep blew away the accumulated grit in a powdery cloud, wiped the neck of the bottle and extracted the cork with a jack-screw opener. He presented the liquor with a beaming countenance. *"La primera tiquilla en todo Mejico, señores."*

"Says it's the best tequilla in all Mexico," Davey told the others. He reached for the offered glass, the rest of the gang doing likewise. Riney, his face arranged to register appreciation of a premium beverage, took a deep draught, rolled it around on his tongue a moment and swallowed it. His eyes watered and he winced at the rawness of the tequilla, then the wince turned to a cough that gradually subsided into a gasp. He looked levelly into the eyes of the barkeep.

"Yeah. Sure it is. I'd hate to see the worst. How about a little Overholt's rye?" The barman immediately bent to select another bottle. It wasn't Overholt's, but definitely rye whiskey. While he did, Riney spoke in a rough, jailhouse whisper, lips not moving. "Watch it! He understands English."

Riney's comment and the bartender's actions drew knowing nods from the gang. When the partly filled bottle rested on the bar, dusted off and opened invitingly, Riney grabbed it and his glass and led the way to a table out of earshot of the *cantinero*. When everyone had drawn up a chair, Riney spoke in a quiet tone:

"Davey, I want you to make a scout of the town. In particular check the layout of the jail. We're gonna have to spring Charlie outta there and do it soon."

"Right, boss." Davey downed a second shot of tequilla and rose, scraped back the gaily painted hand-carved chair and walked to the door. Behind him, Riney continued in a louder voice:

"How about a few hands of stud, boys? Don't seem to be much else to do in this town."

In the jail office, rather than his more comfortable accommodations next door in the *Edificio Municipal*, chief of police, Ruben Padilla, sat behind the desk, a cup of rich, milk-laced chocolate steaming in one hand. With the gringo prisoner to guard until the time of his execution, he felt his presence important. The trial had gone well, if predictably so.

Panchito, tears coursing down his soft young cheeks, had made an excellent witness. In a near whisper he had related the assault on his person, his father's attempted intervention, and the brutal murder. No other witnesses were called. The gringo, the *bandido*, had given his own version, through an interpreter, but the stolid, grim-faced jury of six men from Montenegro had not been moved. They retired to deliberate for a remarkably short ten minutes and returned with a verdict of guilty. Old, gray-haired, *juez* Gonzaga had solemnly accepted their decision and in somber tones sentenced the man to hang. Predictable as he, *jefe* Padilla, had said. Even now a scaffold was being erected in the large courtyard of the municipal building. At dawn tomorrow, *ziiiit*! The gringo would be gone. Padilla sighed his satisfaction and took a deep sip of his chocolate. He leaned back in his chair and threw one booted foot up on his desk. With elaborate care he lighted a small, thin cigar, then looked up, alert, at the sound of a small child's voice calling from outside:

"El jefe! El jefe!"

Ruben Padilla responded to the call, recognizing the voice. *"Sí.* I am inside, Panchito. Come on in."

Panchito, his bruises showing plainly, one grayish bandage covering a shaved patch above his right ear, entered at a run. He stopped before the chief's desk and snatched the straw sombrero from his head.

"*Jefe*. There are five bad men in town, friends of the one that murdered my father." The boy pointed out the open door, across the plaza toward the row of cantinas flanking the main street. "Right now they are at the Cantina Rosales drinking. You will do something, no?"

Padilla half rose from his chair, then reseated himself. "Naturally I will, Panchito, if they are truly here because of the gringo we are going to hang. But first, tell me more about them. What makes you so certain they are friends of this gringo, Bell?"

The boy, still carried away by the scene that had occurred during his father's funeral procession, made an impassioned reply, colored by his youth and the emotional storm, which had raged through him since the previous day. "Why else would such men come to Montenegro? They are mean looking, like the gringo murderer. Giant devils, five of them. As we took my father to his grave they rode into town. They insulted my mother and *Padre* Julio. And they told the *padre* and me that they are devils. I . . . I believe them."

Jefe Padilla nodded solemnly, the hand holding his cigar masking his mouth to conceal a small smile. Then he sobered and continued in a serious vein:

"I do not doubt that. And now, you say they are at the Cantina Rosales. I think . . . " He rose from behind the desk and strapped on his holster belt. "Indeed we shall do something about this. Now, run on home, Panchito."

Late afternoon sun slanted through the dust and

grease-coated windows of the Cantina Rosales. Small motes, disturbed by the hot, lazy breeze, drifted upward to dissipate in the smoke-filled air. A stack of dirty dishes rested on the table where the gang had sat, attesting to their recent meal. Riney and his men stood at the bar now, backs to the beaded glass curtain that covered the opening created by the tall, paneled double doors. From the back room the bartender's voice could be heard scolding his kitchen girl to hurry with a plate of fruit she was working on. Riney and Perk turned abruptly, hands going to their sixguns, at the sound of footsteps pounding on the boardwalk outside. They relaxed when Marv Hoyle entered.

"Hey, Perk, you were sure right about that mañana business!" The collective frowns of the gang quieted the rest of Marv's report. "Those Mezkin soldiers made camp for the night not ten miles outside town. We can easily overtake them and be to the canyon first." Marv looked away from Riney to each of the others, seeking support. "We'll even have time to get ol' Charlie free."

"You did a good job, Marv." Riney gave grudging praise. "Now come on up and have a drink an' we'll talk about it."

Marv joined the gang and accepted a glass of tequilla from Davey. The bartender appeared in the inner doorway, bearing a large platter filled with slices of apple, jicama, and bananas, seasoned lightly with a mild chili powder, lime juice, and grated coconut. "Here, *señores*, a few *bocadillos* to increase the enjoyment of your drinking. Compliments of the Cantina Rosales."

"Mighty nice of you," Davey replied after translating the barkeep's words for the gang. He started to turn, then froze, his hand darting toward his holster.

"No, *señor!* That would be a . . . how you say? . . . fatal mistake." The rattling of beads announced Padilla's entrance to the barroom. He held a double barrel shotgun at waist level, centered on Davey's middle. He kept his eyes on Davey while he addressed the others.

"That's right, hombres. All of you stand as you are. Please to put your hands out on the bar. I do not wish trouble, however I came prepared." Padilla sidestepped to allow a uniformed policeman to enter. The cop carried a heavy Colt's Dragoon pistol, which he cocked menacingly, hate glittering in his slitted ebony eyes.

Padilla spoke again as he strode cat-footed toward the bar. "It seems we have a friend of yours as our guest." He *tisked* sympathetically. "It would be too much a shame were he to depart before tomorrow's festivities." Padilla stopped at one end of the line, his hand outstretched toward Marv.

"To insure he stays here for his hanging, you, *señores*, will now give me all of your weapons. You first, *poco mozo*." He spat the insulting term for "little boy" at Marv. "Step out so you can be searched."

Marv shot a quizzical glance at Riney, who nodded slowly and winked with his off-eye, out of the sight of the Mexican policeman. Marv stepped forward and submitted to having his pistol removed. The *jefe* handed it to his police officer and began to pat Marv down. Unseen by either lawman, Riney, who was next to be searched, slipped a knife from his boot top. A small, narrow stiletto, it fit invisibly in the palm of his hand. He passed it to Davey, who stood next to him. Davey, in turn, handed it on to Pearly. The *jefe* finished his search of Marv and stepped up to Riney.

"No doubt you are famous *bandidos* in your own country, *verdad?* And perhaps there are even large rewards on your heads. Alas, they cannot be collected here in Montenegro. Therefore, once we have insured your peaceful intentions, you shall not be further disturbed." He finished with Riney and motioned to Davey. "Now you, *Indio*. Step out here."

Davey complied and Padilla removed the Dragoon, scalping knife and a large hunting knife from Davey's belt. He also took a Model 3 Colt derringer from Davey's boot top. Padilla completed his search, and Davey stepped back into line. Before his summons came, Pearly slipped the knife back to Davey. Quickly the Mexican policemen finished their examination and gathered up the weapons. Padilla loaded them into the arms of his officer. Slowly, they began backing to the doorway.

"Pardon us for this small interruption, gentlemen. You are welcome to stay in Montenegro as long as you wish. As to your weapons, you may have them back tomorrow . . . right after we hang your friend. Now, good afternoon." Padilla released the hammers on his shotgun, turned and started out the door in the wake of his overburdened policeman. In so doing, he made the one error the gang hoped for.

Davey took a single step away from the bar, drew back his hand, fingers lightly clinched on the blade of the stiletto. He threw with a smooth, even follow through, the slender knife making a faint whirring through the air before it struck Ruben Padilla in the back.

The blade sank nearly to the hilt alongside the *jefe's* spine. Padilla staggered, gasped softly and fell, half turning, to land back inside the the cantina. The clatter of his dropped shotgun sounded loudly in the silent saloon.

On the sidewalk, the policeman reacted to the unexpected noise. He rushed inside to find his *jefe* lying partway on his back in a pool of spreading blood. All thought of the outlaws forgotten, he rushed to his chief's side, dropped his collection of arms and knelt. He turned Padilla over, to reveal the knife buried between his shoulder blades. Astonished, the cop looked up for the first time to find the source of the stiletto that had so miraculously appeared. His eyes widened in horror, and he raised a trembling arm in a feeble attempt to ward off the descending blow.

The chair in Perk Perkins's hands split apart upon contact with the policeman's head. It fell away to reveal a deep, blood-gushing cleft in the top of his skull. Immediately the gang rushed over and rearmed themselves. Behind them the thoroughly frightened bartender crossed himself twice and murmured to one in particular, *"Madre de Cristo!"*

Perk's sensitive ears caught the sound, though, and he whirled back to the saloon keeper. "You get down behind that bar of yourn and don't move for half an hour. Ya hear?"

"Sí, señor." The barman made haste to reply. He ducked behind the counter out of sight, whimpered slightly and once more made the sign of the cross. The gang hurried to the door and out onto the boardwalk.

"Perk, you take our horses around behind the jail," Riney ordered as he pointed the direction. "There's one down there we'll bring for Charlie. Davey, you an' Marv come with me. Pearly, you go with Perk and set me a two stick charge. Now, move!"

In a few minutes, no sign of the outlaws remained. The siesta-quieted streets of Montenegro returned almost to normal.

Chapter 8

In the cottonwood-shaded draw where Riney Stark and his gang had camped on the night before Charlie's debacle in Montenegro, *Natana-jo* reined his pony and slid from its back. He walked to where his chief scout squatted, digging a stick into a buried fire pit.

"They camp here, two, three suns ago, old friend. Only five." He pointed to a distant spot. "One man, one horse go away, not return."

Natana-jo pondered this information. Why had the murdering white-eyes ridden further into Mexico? Would they go to the big village beyond the hills? Were they aware that he and his men followed them? These questions would require much thought.

"We camp here tonight," he told the braves. "Go on when our father the sun comes in the morning. Rest . . . eat . . . soon the *Pen-dik-olye* will be in our hands."

Riney and Davey approached the jail the long way, around two sides of the square. Riney held their horses while Davey stepped quietly to the door. The half-breed pounded loudly on the thick wooden panel, waited, then pounded again.

"*Quien es?*" a voice called from inside.

"*Manuel. Abreme, por favor!*"

Inside, the jailer rose from his chair, a sixgun in one hand. A puzzled frown creased his smooth brow. Which Manuel did the man outside mean? And why should he open the door until the *jefe* returned, as his instructions had told him? He moved cautiously to the heavy oak partition and slid back a small flap over a peephole. He could see no one. In order to fulfil his duties conscientiously, he pressed his face to the eyepiece and peered out.

Davey Two-Knife shoved the muzzle of his Dragoon into the space between two wrought-iron bars on the peephole and fired instantly. The shot caught the jailer in his right eye socket, blasting through brain matter and crashing out the back of his skull, taking great gouts of tissue, blood, and bone with it. The dead man fell backward without a sound.

Riney stepped forward and jerked at Davey's sleeve. "Come on, let's get movin'."

Around behind the jail, Riney handed the reins of their horses to Marv, who stood off to one side, holding those of the other outlaws. Riney stepped quietly to the narrow, barred window of a cell. The sun was setting, and long, black shadows fell across Montenegro. Riney stood on tiptoe and whispered hoarsely.

"Charlie? You there, boy?"

Charlie Bell, startled by the gunshot out front, sat upright on his bunk, clutching a thin blanket to his chest. His eyes rolled wildly in their sockets, and he imagined that at any minute a raving lynch mob would pour down the small corridor and throw open his cell.

The sound of Riney's voice made him jump. He yelped in fear, then recovered himself.

"Th-that you, Riney? Is it?"

From outside, Charlie heard the faintly mocking voice of Perk Perkins. "That's him, all right, Riney."

Charlie rushed to the slit window, wrapping pale knuckles around the bars. His voice bubbled with relief and released tension. "It's you, boss? For sure? Man oh man, am I glad to hear from you. I thought it was a greaser lynch mob."

His voice changed when he realized that the gunshot, which had killed the jailer, had been fired by his friends, not men bent on hanging him. "What you go an' kill that dumb jailer for, Riney? How you gonna get me out now? You can see the winder's too little. Riney? Answer me. You ain't mad at me, are you?"

"Hell yes, I'm mad at you!" Riney snapped. "Now, if you'll shut up long enough I'll tell you what I'm gonna do."

"You are gonna get me out, ain't you, boss?"

"Put a cinch on that big mouth of yours, Charlie, or I won't. Pearly, you set that charge?"

"All ready when you want it, Riney."

A low whimper came from inside the jail. "Now, Charlie, listen to me. And you better listen carefully. You got a mattress in that cell?"

Charlie's slowly dawning realization of how they planned to effect his escape from jail sounded clearly in his voice. "I—I got a couple greasy rags stuffed with straw, Riney. B-but . . . what you say about . . . a, ah, charge? You ain't gonna blast me out, are you?"

Riney let the raw edged of his growing exasperation enter the tone of his voice. "Hush up and listen! Now, you take that mattress of yours and get down in a corner as far from this wall as you can get. Sink down real low and cover up with all the paddin' you have. That clear?"

"S-sure it is. But, ah, Riney," Charlie protested feebly. "Blastin' powder?"

Impatient with Charlie's continual whining, Riney turned to Pearly. "Light the fuse."

Suddenly panic burst in Charlie and he cried out hastily. "All right, all right! I'll get down! Just wait a minute, will you?"

Perk came forward with a pick in his hand. "I found this pick over there."

Pearly, as the expert powder man, took command. "Good, dig a hole right . . . there." When Perk bent to his task, Pearly turned to call out softly to Marv. "Marv, toss me one o' them canteens. I gotta mix a little mud." He set to work, one eye on Perk's efforts. When the hole looked deep enough he signaled a halt. Pearly bent low and inserted the small bundle of blasting powder sticks into the cavity, then packed it closed with the thick mud he'd mixed.

"You ready, Charlie?" Pearly asked in a whisper.

"You sure there's no other way?" Charlie's voice came faintly to them from where he crouched under the filthy, louse-infested mattress.

"Hold them horses," Riney commanded Marv. "Right enough, Pearly. Let 'er go!"

A match flared in the darkening alley, and Pearly touched it to the frayed end of the waterproof fuse. It sputtered briefly and then released a steady, hissing shower of sparks while it burned the short distance to the explosive. The gang rushed away from the beseiged wall.

Two seconds later a bright flash illuminated the narrow passage.

Immediately a dull, flat roar assailed their eardrums, and the air filled with a huge brown dust cloud. Following a fraction of a second later, the ground jolted violently, and the horses whinnied in fear while the tremors subsided. The outlaws rushed to the gaping hole in the adobe wall. From inside they heard a fit of spasmodic coughing.

"You all right, Charlie?" Riney called.

Charlie raced out of the swirling dust and powder smoke, which filled the cell. He nearly collided with the gang leader. Charlie gagged and flailed at the dust, then bowled on past, to stop only when he crashed into the broad chest of the stamping horse.

"Oh my God! I . . . I cain't hear a thing. I cain't even hear myself. I'm deaf for life. Riney, where are you? Help me!"

"Open your eyes, idjit!" Perk growled. Pearly, Marv, and Riney had bent double with laughter at the sight of their rescued friend. Perk joined them with a thick guffaw and lapsed into a giggle while he continued. " 'Pears to me as how anyone who got shut of hearin' you for life could count it as a blessin'."

"What? What's that you say, Perk?"

Perk glowered at Charlie. "Ah, shut up, will ya?"

"All right, boys. Let's mount up and ride," Riney ordered.

Riney Stark raised his hand in a signal to halt. He reined his horse sideways atop the long ridge outside

Montenegro and waited while the others clustered around.

"Well, boys, we'd best light out for that canyon."

Charlie, whose hearing had only partially returned, peered curiously at the gang leader. "We still goin' after that silver?"

"Sure, Charlie. You got anything else to do? Your dance card all filled up?"

Charlie pushed out his lower lip in a pink pout. "You're funnin' me again, Riney. But what about all them *federales*? Won't they do somethin' when they know I got busted outta jail?"

"You can bet on it, Charlie. Them Mezkin soldier cops will be quick on our trail when they find out what happened back there. Way I've got it figgered, we can take care of them and get the silver easy."

Charlie beamed his idiot grin. "Sure we can. But how?"

"Simple. With those soldier boys out of the way, the wagons will be unguarded. We can scoop up all the silver bars we can carry and just ride off."

"Right. So we're gonna leave a nice clear trail from here to that there canyon and wait for the *federales* to follow it. Ride out."

Raul Lowery, son of an Irish mining engineer and Mexican mother, sat astride his mount, his chest swelled with pride. A captain at only twenty-five and leader of a crack troop of *federales*, he was entrusted with the important assignment of transporting five million pesos in silver from the treasury at *Ciudad Mexico* to the state governor in Chihuahua City. How magnificent he and his *soldados* looked in their green, red, and white uniforms with the lacy braid and flashy gold buttons.

Their cockaded "water-pail" shakoes with the black feather plumes bobbed gayly in the warm morning air. They should have worn, he knew, their service uniforms of chocolate-colored charro sombreros, pants and vests of the same hue, and pale buff shirts with rough-out boots, in this land of tans and browns. But the dress costume seemed more suited to the mission, Raul believed. Then, in the middle of the night, the situation had changed.

In their camp they had heard the dull rumble of an explosion in the distance, toward Montenegro. Raul had dismissed it, considering it unworthy of his time in light of the task given his troop. Then the alcalde and two men of substance in the city had ridden into their bivouac on lathered horses, their eyes big and round with fear.

They had told him of the gringo scheduled to be hanged and of his friends who had come to town; the chief of police and two policemen murdered and the back wall of the jail blown out with blasting powder. The alcalde had implored him, begged him to come to their aid.

"But surely, *Señor* Alcalde, you must realize," Raul had protested. "Our prime mission is to protect the silver shipment you see in those wagons."

"Your *prime* mission is to protect the citizens of Mexico, *Señor Capitán*," the mayor had retorted in an acid tone. "How can we, or the silver be safe with these devils on the loose? If you pursue these gringo *ladrones* now, *immediamente*, you can deal with them most sharply and still deliver your silver quite safely, to the state capital."

"It is beyond my consideration, *señor*," Raul had blustered.

"It is your only consideration, *capitán*. We . . . and you . . . are at their mercy unless they are apprehended swiftly and given over to the hangman. If I must, I shall accompany you to the capital and present my case to representative of the central government, along with your refusal to come to our aid."

"Do you threaten me?"

"I only wish to show you the alternatives, *Señor Capitán*."

The argument waxed on until at last Raul relented. He organized pursuit early in the morning, and they set out at dawn. The foolish gringos had left a trail childishly simple to follow. Now, the sharp edges and depth of the tracks indicated they had but a short way to go to close with their enemy. Raul rose in the stirrups, affecting to peer into the hazy distance, but actually to ease his aching knees and thighs. What was that? There on the horizon. A dark smudge in the unrelenting buff of a high plateau?

Another ten minutes' gallop and Raul clearly made out the wide entrance to a high-walled canyon. That must be *Cañon Diablo*, he thought, making a mental check of the maps carried by his sergeant. A most fitting place to come to grips with the gringo *bandidos*. He turned to shout over his shoulder.

"Trumpeter forward!"

The bugler jumped his horse to a faster pace and pulled alongside his commanding officer. The youth, a boy of fourteen, took soldiering seriously and felt a quickening in his heart at the prospect of battle. He held his shiny brass instrument at the ready and looked earnestly at Raul for his orders. "*Sí, mí capitán?*"

"Stay at my side. See that canyon ahead? If I have any reasoning power at all, the gringos will be trapped inside, and we shall soon annihilate them."

"*Magnifico*! When do you wish me to sound the charge?"

"The moment we see them, Ricardo. The peal of the trumpet and the sight of our lances, our flying pennants, our splendid uniforms, should put the fear of God into the gringos, and they shall fall to us with ease."

"*Muy suerte, mí capitán.*"

"Great luck, indeed, Ricardo. Six gringos against a troop of *federales*? They would need the very best of all luck to successfully oppose us."

Raul, his sabre drawn, led his men more than halfway into *Cañon Diablo* with no sight of the fleeing *bandidos*. He felt a stab of doubt assail his confidence that he had judged the gringos correctly. He turned in his saddle, on the point of ordering a halt, when the air ripped apart in a cacophony of unbearable noise, while blast after blast rippled along the canyon walls high above their heads. Great waves of loose shale cascaded down to bury men and horses alike.

Huge, bounding boulders joined in the dusty, clamoring onslaught, bouncing heavenward, to descend like celestial cannonballs on the soft flesh of soldier and animal. One giant stone smashed into the hindquarters of Raul's mount, driving horse and rider to the ground. Faintly he heard his trumpeter wildly playing the signal for recall and then regroup in the instant before another half-ton behemoth landed on his skull and squashed it to a forthy pink pulp. Gunfire crackled along the column, growing to a sustained fusillade, and the ambushed troopers realized with horror that the battle had only begun.

Riney Stark watched the garishly uniformed *federales* thunder into the canyon, and his face lit with a smile of satisfaction. He and the others crouched behind obscuring boulders midway along the canyon walls, each holding in one hand a cluster of fuses, cut to various lengths, a ready match in the other. When Riney saw the troops reach the midpoint of the rubble-strewn floor, he gave the signal, struck his lucifer and touched off his five powder trains.

Once the blast had buffeted their ears with dreadful punishment and the shale and boulders had plummeted down to unhorse and destroy many of the *federales*, they came from hiding and, with wild rebel yells, charged downhill amid the last fine cobbles of the landslide. Their revolvers blazed to each side and ahead of them, accounting for more of the hapless troopers. Marv and Perk were first to dash in among the downed Mexican soldiers, their sixguns crashing and spitting leaden death to those who showed the slightest indication of life.

Marv dismounted beside little Ricardo, the trumpeter, and reached out to jerk back his head by his long, black hair. Grinning, Marv shoved the muzzle of his Merwin and Hulbertson into the pale face of the Mexican boy and started to pull the trigger.

The shot blasted loudly in a momentary lull in

battle.

A huge cloud of powder smoke momentarily obscured both lads, then Marv toppled backward and fell dead on the scattered shale, eyes staring sightlessly, mouth agape, his chest shot away by the boy soldier's huge Dragoon pistol. The gang had little time to take note as firing broke out again all along the line.

Riney and Davey took cool aim, dispatching a man or animal with each round fired. Pearly, enormously pleased with the effectiveness of his carefully calculated series of blasts, bounded down the slope, a blazing sixgun in each hand, casually plinking at moving green uniforms like empty whiskey bottles floating on the stream on a Sunday afternoon. On the opposite side of the canyon floor, Perk Perkins hummed "Lorena," while using his Sharps to disintegrate the heads of any *federales* brazen enough to expose themselves to him. The gang's infernal work continued for over five minutes.

Then, suddenly as it had begun, the fight ended.

Only Charlie Bell still shot at their enemy, pumping bullets into the unresisting corpses of the *federales*. He limped and held one hand over a slightly bleeding wound in his left buttock. All the while he shouted at the corpses he assaulted:

"Damn-blasted greasers! Shoot Charlie Bell in the ass will you? I'll show you, I'll show you!" Charlie continued to load and fire while the gang gathered silently around him.

"All right, Charlie," Riney called tonelessly. "They're all dead now. You can quit shootin' at 'em."

Charlie looked up a moment, an insane grin on his face. "Don't know about that, Riney. Shouldn't we shoot 'em some more, huh? Maybe some of 'em's playin' possum, like that little 'Pache brat."

"You fixin' to scalp them, too, Charlie?" Pearly asked, a note of scorn in his voice.

"Black hair's black hair, ain't it? All looks alike when you go to sell it."

The gang members looked incredulously at Charlie, and Perk shook his head in disgust. "Sometimes I think there's somethin' mighty wrong with you, Charlie."

"Aw, Perk, what causes you to say that?" Charlie's Remington barked again. It caused dust and shreds of cloth to fly from a dead *federale's* green jacket. "There! Ya see that one? See him?" Charlie yelled, his voice warm with vindication.

Pearly's lips twisted with distaste. "He was dead, Charlie. Just as dead as Marv."

Charlie's face changed, lost its kill fever. "Marv? One o' these greasers did in Marv? Why, that's downright awful."

"Sure is," Pearly agreed. "Seein' as how he's the one knew all about Colby. Wonder how far it is from here?"

Riney stepped up, ejecting empty cylinders from his Navy Colts and inserting fresh ones. "We can worry about that later. Now, let's get our cayuses and light out for that silver train. It's ours for the takin'."

Chapter 9

Large, black turkey buzzards, their bellies bloated from gorging on the gory remains in *Cañon Diablo*, flapped their wings lazily and rose into the air, indifferent to the arrival of *Natana-jo* and his warriors. They had trailed Stark's gang from their last campsite to this place of death and destruction, guided the remaining few miles by the gathering of the winged scavengers. Even to such fierce and savage fighters as these Apache braves, the scene of carnage enveloped them in awe. They clustered close together, unspeaking, and sat motionless on their horses. At last their leader slipped from his pony's back.

"This is the work of those who raided our village," *Natana-jo* declared in a positive manner. "They are truly fiends, demon spirits from that dark place beneath our mother the earth. Come, take the firesticks of the *soldados*. Those we cannot use, we can trade."

A moment later, one of the warriors cried out in excited triumph. "*Natana-jo*! Here, come to me. See, see this one. The *Me-ji-kanos* fought bravely. They have killed one of the demons."

The Apache war chief hurried to where the man knelt beside the body of Marv Hoyle. A white-eye, yes. Young, by the looks of him. *Natana-jo* motioned for his chief scout to join them. The wrinkled face puckered in concentration while Satanta bent to examine the corpse. He peered longest at Marv's boots.

"Ha! Yes, this is one of those we seek. See here, the arrowhead notch in his boot sole. He walked among our *wikiups*, brought death to our women and children. To look at this tells me that this one," he said pointing to the dead trumpeter, "the small boy *Me-ji-kano* killed him. That is just."

"Your eyes see truth, Satanta. It is good as you say. Now, go and find the way taken by these dark ones. Soon they shall taste our vengeance."

Two hours later the Apache warriors came upon the ill-fated silver train. Dead horses lay in the traces, the bodies of several men scattered about, bloating in the sun of midday. The survivors, some wounded, all crazed by thirst, were too feeble to put up resistance when they saw their dreaded enemy, the Apache, ride quietly in among them. *Natana-jo* and his lifelong friend, Satanta, studied the scene while the braves pillaged the wagons, uncovering the remaining silver ingots. The war chief sighed heavily, his eyes filled with smoldering anger.

"Like these men thirst for water, those we seek have a thirst for death that cannot be quenched." The chief spoke in a near philosophical mood. "If the Spirits will it, we shall thrust that craving back down their throats."

"Yes. But when, old friend?"

"Tomorrow, Satanta, or the next day, or the one after

that."

Although silver had no use among the Apache, *Natana-jo* knew well its value in dealing with the Mexicans and Americans. He gave brisk orders to his men to take two bars each. When they had complied with his command and sat their mounts, ready to ride on, *Natana-jo* contemplated the small band of survivors, herded together in the shade of one wagon. They had no animals and were not trained like the Apache to cover great distances on foot. Many would die of their wounds. All would perish from thirst. But slowly — and ever so painfully.

To his way of seeing things, *Natana-jo* acted out of compassion when he ordered them slain quickly, with merciful blows.

When the act had been completed and the last dying moan faded on the wind, *Natana-jo* waved one bronze, muscular arm above his head in a circular motion. "Come. We ride after the demons."

A brassy, white-hot sun burned down from a sky faded pale like an old work shirt, stifling the activities of even the daytime lizards of the Chihuahua desert. The gang's greed, following their lightning raid on the silver wagons, worked to their disadvantage. Six bars each, one hundred twenty pounds of silver per man, taxed their horses to the extreme. They walked now, leading their flagging mounts. Each man's clothes showed dark circles around armpits, necks, and waists. At last Riney called a halt.

"This ain't gonna do it, boys. We're about to drop, an' our horses won't do another mile. I say we have to bury the silver, come back for it later."

"But where, Riney?" Pearly asked plaintively. "There's nothin' around here but sand and cactus. We'd never find it again."

"We'll bury it, nevertheless." Riney looked around in a wide circle. "Over there. See those rocks? If we're careful, nobody will ever know it's there but us."

"How we gonna tell that bunch o' rocks from any other, Riney?" Charlie Bell moaned.

"That's easy enough, Charlie." Riney opened the flap of his left-hand saddlebag and brought out a compass and a small note pad. He first oriented himself and then took a bearing on a small, red-ochre butte, standing apart from several others on the horizon ahead of them. He made a crude map of the area and the placed an X at the location he presumed them to occupy. Then he noted the reading for the butte. Next Riney turned and took a bearing on the rocks. Entering this information on his chart, he pocketed the compass and took his reins again, leading out toward the cluster of boulders.

Once they reached their goal, Riney took another bearing on the distant butte and included it on the map. Then he searched the area for a suitable location. One huge boulder caught his eye. Wind and sand eroded to form an overhang. It had a large pile of lesser stones at its base.

"That's it, boys. Move them rocks, dig a hole and we'll put the silver in there. Then we cover it all back the way it was, wipe out any traces of our bein' here and ride on to Colby."

"Ah, Colby," Perk remarked wistfully. "I wonder if we'll ever really get to see that burg?"

A light scudding of early morning clouds evaporated away in the heat of the rising sun that warmed Colby, New Mexico to wakefulness and another day. Roosters, eternally deceived by false dawn, ruffled their feathers in confusion and crowed a second time, disturbed, as always, by this interruption of their orderly routine. Here and there kerosene lamps winked out, and men in shirt-sleeves or vests emerged from houses, donning their coats against the residual night chill lingering among the buildings.

In a short while the bell outside the weather-beaten, sagging-roofed, one room schoolhouse would be rung by scrawny, pop-eyed old Orsen Larabe, the prissy schoolmaster, summoning a flock of tassel-headed, yelling imps from the warmth of their mothers' kitchens to the rigors of the three R's. Howard Wilkins, his mind still dwelling on his recent reflections of his life in Colby, completed his daybreak ritual like all the others. This morning Amy had risen early, dressed and made ready to accompany Howie to the general mercantile. The only exception to this time-worn skein of events was Marshal Clint Rider.

Clint had been up and about his rounds a good four hours before the other citizens of Colby. He strode along Main Street, checking doorknobs, peering down alleyways and extinguishing the occasional street lamp that had not been quenched after closing time for the saloons. As usual, he timed his progress so that he stood opposite Wilkins's mercantile when Howie and Amy rounded the far corner. Clint felt a warm smile of genuine friendliness crease his sun-leathered cheeks when he stepped off the boardwalk to cross the dusty street. He reached the far side at the precise moment the Wilkinses paused so that Howie could unlock the door. Clint tipped his hat and spoke with his customary slow drawl:

"Mornin' Miz Wilkins . . . Howie."

Amy seemed determined to make the best of this daily encounter for once. "Yes it is. And a fine morning to you, too, marshal."

"Mornin' to you, Clint. Pass a peaceable night?" Howie had abandoned his efforts on the lock to look at his friend and engaged in their daily ritual. Amy's impatience with the two men crept to the surface in the form of a rhythmic foot tapping. Already her resolve had weakened.

"Peaceable as usual, Howie. 'Tweren't no trouble to speak of." Clint broke off to remove his hat and study the sky as though seeking portents from the Almighty. "Looks like another scorcher today."

Howie also inspected the sky. "Reckon as how you're right, Clint. Gettin' to be one right after another, seems. Mighty good fishin' weather, though."

Clint consulted the liner of his Stetson in the manner of an actor peeking at cue cards for his missing lines. "Would be, if it weren't too hot for the fish to bite."

Amy's foot taps had grown louder, and Clint smiled shyly when they reached his consciousness. He replaced the hat on his head and changed his mood abruptly.

"Well, gotta finish my mornin' rounds. I'll drop by later. Have a nice day." He touched two fingers to the brim in salute. "Howie . . . ma'am."

Howie turned the key in the lock, held the door for

his wife to enter ahead of him, then turned back to raise the narrow green shades that obscured the tall glass panels in the upper half. Amy flounced to the counter, turned abruptly on her husband with a sour face, her earlier good humor banished.

"How-ard! He's at it again. So help me I can't endure it another day. 'Have a nice day,' she mimicked in a passable imitation of Clint's drawl. "Aaagh! As if anyone could have a nice day in this . . . this end-of-the-line town."

"Now, now, my dear," Howie placated. "You'll forget all about it before noon. This is egg day, remember? All the wives will be coming in to bring their week's gathering. You'll have lots of nice company."

"If those biddies' incessant, meaningless gossip doesn't bore me to death, you mean."

Outside, Clint winced sympathetically for his friend's misfortune and made his way back across the street. He turned the white ceramic knob on the cafe door and entered. Clint glanced up at the hexagonal-faced pendulum clock that hung on the wall above the potbelly stove and nodded with satisfaction. Seven-thirty. He was right on time. He took a stool at the counter, in front of an empty ashtray, and looked up with a generous smile for the attractively built, but plain-looking woman in her mid-thirties, who came from the back room to serve him.

"Just coffee, Dorie. I can't stay long." Clint took out the makings and rolled himself a cigarette. He touched a match to the tip, inhaled deeply and contentedly sighed out the smoke. Clint's other hand reached for the steaming cup of brew that Dorie deposited before him. He'd enjoy it while he could, Clint decided. He hadn't long to spare.

The clock on the wall behind Clint's broad shoulders read ten-ten when he stood to leave. The ashtray beside his hand overflowed with crushed butts. Clint hitched up his gun belt and turned toward the doorless entrance to the kitchen.

"Well, sittin' here don't get my work done. Obliged for the good coffee, Dorie."

"My pleasure, Clint. You be in for dinner?"

"What's fixin'?"

"Chicken and noodles."

"My favorite. Purely the food of the gods, Dorie. Count on me. Be here at noon on the dot."

Clint stepped out onto the boardwalk and started off toward the marshal's office and jail a block away and around the corner from the bank. He paused at the rumble of wagon wheels squealing out their need for a proper greasing. Clint turned back, more to verify his guess than satisfy curiosity.

A buckboard, pulled by a bony pair of bays, came to a stop in front of Howie's store. Seated on the leaf-spring mounted bench were Fred Simpson and his wife, Nel. At the back, bare feet hanging over the tailgate, were the Simpson children, a towheaded boy of eleven and a girl about seven. Clint congratulated himself on the accuracy of his surmise, though he felt a twinge of pity for the family's poverty. Their clothes, well worn, faded and much patched, but clean, attested to the folly of dirt farming in a desert climate. There'd always be those stubborn or foolish enough to try it, though, Clint salved his conscience. Fred Simpson waved to the marshal, and Clint crossed the street to greet them.

"Howdy, Fred, Miz Simpson. In for the monthly shoppin'?"

"How do, marshal. Yep, we're bringin' in some cream for Dorie at the cafe, and the missus has her eggs for Howie. Thought we'd pick up a few things we needed while we was here."

"An' some rock candy, huh, Paw?" Tommy Simpson piped up from the back of the wagon.

"We'll see about that, young man," Nel Simpson interposed. "There's not too many pennies to be spared for frivolities in these hard times."

"Now, Mother," Fred chided gently. "The younguns is entitled to at least a penny's worth of fun outtin' a whole month's time, ain't they?"

Nel Simpson made as if to reply, then held her tongue when Fred stepped down and helped her from the seat. Clint walked to the rear and hoisted Tommy high in the air, bringing a shout of delight from the boy. He next did the same for the lad's sister, who squealed and giggled and hugged the big, rugged marshal enthusiastically. Clint tipped his hat and walked on.

Inside the mercantile, Nel Simpson went directly to the counter where Amy, a feather duster in one hand, held court. The children dashed to a place before the large glass jars of licorice whips, horehound drops, rock crystal candy, and other delights, their eyes wide with fascination and yearning. Their father walked to where Howie stood on a ladder, back to the door, placing boxes of .44 Winchester cartridges on a high shelf. Fred reached behind the counter and brought out a checkerboard. He placed it on a nail keg that sat between two captain's chairs by the stove. He took his place in one while Howie climbed down from his perch.

"Mornin', Howie."

"Mornin', Fred."

"Your move as I recollect, Howie."

"That's right, Fred." Howie studied the board for a moment, then moved a piece, jumping two of Fred's tokens.

"You ain't been studyin' that board, have you?"

"You know better than that, Fred."

"I know you're a man of your word, Howie, but sometimes a temptation rears its ugly head."

"I haven't looked at this board for a whole month."

"I didn't say you had looked at it, Howie. I jist feel . . . well, like I said, temptation."

"Are we gonna play checkers or talk about temptation all day?" After Howie's declaration, the two players fell to a concentrated silence. Over at the counter, Amy displayed for Nel's consideration a lovely dress, cut in the most recent eastern fashion. It was a frilly, gossamer thing, totally useless for frontier life.

"Now, look at this, Nel. Why, with this dress you'd be the envy of everyone at the church socials. This is the finest material to come from St. Louis."

"Don't take me wrong, Amy Wilkins. I hold it to be right pretty, true enough, and surely a pride to own. Mind, I don't go many places and my man'd whale the tar outta me if I spent so much on a doodad like this. Why, we need so many other things first."

"Surely he wants you to have nice things, Nel. Besides, what can be more important to a woman than bein' prettied up now and then?"

"Once a month we get in for church and to do the

buyin'. The barn needs a tin roof. We gotta have salt cakes and some grain for the cows about to drop a calf. And my man needs new galluses, a hat. Tommy needs some material for a couple shirts. Land sakes, the boy's goin' without almost every day now, so's he's as brown as an Indian. Growed out of his shoes, too."

An edge of exasperation entered Amy's voice. "Always it's your menfolk! Don't you ever think of yourself first? Don't Fred even care?"

The certain serenity of righteousness touched Nel's face and words, though without malice or smallness. "Ain't so sure that thinkin' of one's self first's not a sin. And, like they say, a woman's job is to care for her man. 'Sides, Fred bought me a dress not long ago, right pretty one, too. Best one I ever had. Still is. It was the year after Tommy was born."

Amy's eyes flew wide with shock. She couldn't believe what she'd heard. How could any woman, no matter how mean the circumstances of her upbringing and life, tolerate such a dreary, unfair situation.

"Why . . . that was ten years ago, Nel! I'd not stand for such treatment, were I you. Why, I'd not have a thing if I waited for Howie to notice I needed it." She gulped in breath to summon strength behind her lordly, superior pronouncement.

"We women gotta take the lead, make the men do as they should."

Nel's shock surpassed that of the outraged Amy. She spoke calmly, though icily.

"Amy, I love my man. The marriage vow says for better or worse, doesn't it? What you suggest . . . it's just not natural. A woman's place is makin' her man happy." A loud clacking of a playing piece repeatedly striking the board and a gleeful shout from Fred Simpson ended his wife's defense of the status quo.

"And that does that, Howie! Half a dollar you owe me."

Howard studied the board, vacant of all black pieces. "Yes . . . that . . . does . . . that, Fred."

"I could have you credit that on my account, Howie. But, I got me a better idee." He raised his voice, head turned toward the two women. "Woman! I won the game. Got me a half dollar cash money from old Howie here. You just buy yourself some pretties with that, ya hear?"

"An' some rock candy, too, Paw?" Tommy asked shyly.

Fred blinked, then grinned and reached out to ruffle his son's mop of blond hair. "And some rock candy for these younguns, too, woman, an' a penny's worth of horehound drops on top of it all."

At this dictum, Nel gave Amy a wise, mature and knowing look. "When you got a good man, you should treat him right, Amy, and he'll treat you right, too." She glanced over Amy's shoulder at a tall shelf, ignoring the younger woman's cold glare. "May I see some of them pretty hair ribbons, Amy?"

Evening came to Colby with the same dreadful regularity of each morning's sunrise. Objects cast their long, black shadows down the street, and the air tinted a deep orange as the sun set in a crimson dust haze. Amy Wilkins waited for her husband on the boardwalk, hands tucked into a lace-covered muff. Howie drew the blinds, closed the door and rattled the huge brass padlock. He snapped it with finality and looked up satisfied. He extended his arm for Amy's support, but she disdained it.

"Evenin', Howie, ma'am." Clint Rider stood in the dust of the street, hat in one hand.

"Evenin', Clint. Pass a peaceable day?"

"Yep, a peaceable day. Looks like we'll get no letup this night," Clint continued, his eyes on the sky.

Howie studied the sky a moment, also. "Yep. Looks like another scorcher tomorrow."

"Hurry, Howie," Amy interrupted in a strained, impatient tone. "It's time to go home. Heavens knows I still have supper to fix, while you can make all the inane—"

"Certainly, my dear." Howie cut her off to avoid the intentional offense she directed at Clint Rider. "Well, Clint, we'd best be gettin' along. A good evenin' to you."

"Evenin', Howie . . . ma'am."

Clint remained standing in the street in front of Howie's store, his eyes on the couple's retreating backs. Amy's jaw waggled in purposeful vehemence, and Clint shook his head regretfully for the burden his friend had to endure. Well, he thought, it's not my cross to bear. One more turn around town before Billy takes over, then off for some cold sliced beef and a beer at the Silver Slipper.

Chapter 10

Pearly Wilson bent close to his image in the small steel mirror that hung in a mesquite bush. His straight-edge razor rasped loudly in the early morning stillness. Always the dandy, Pearly worked fingertips and blade with meticulous care around the pencil line of moustache that adorned his upper lip. He drew one hand, almost contemplatively, along the strong, tanned line of his jaw. The other gang members, less fastidious, made short work of their morning ablutions. All except Charlie.

Charlie industriously polished a pair of gold-rim eyeglasses. When he finished he placed them on the bridge of his nose at a jaunty angle and began to clown in front of the others. He wore a tall, gray, beaver hat, velvet-lapeled cutaway coat of a deep maroon color, tight-fitting, striped trousers and, incongruously, gray spats over his western boots. He capered up to Pearly, appearing behind the outlaw in the mirror.

"Now, my goodness, ain't I just the prettiest thing?"

Perk Perkins looked up from tending a skillet full of fatback over the fire. "You want the truth?"

Pearly stopped shaving and turned to examine the

sartorial splendor. "Where'd you come by that outlandish outfit, Charlie?"

"Found the duds in a valise in one o' them silver wagons. The topper came outta a big leather boxlike thing. Iffin Davey's right, we'll be ridin' into Colby some time today. Thought I'd dress for the occasion. Clothes make the man, don't you know?"

Pearly made a mock serious examination of the ill-fitting costume before him and waved his razor in Charlie's face. "In your case, Charlie, I have my doubts. Looks like you're tricked out for your own funeral. Which makes me think you'd better watch out some townie in Colby don't take a likin' to those fancy duds. He's liable to gun you down for 'em."

Charlie stopped gyrating, and a look of offended dignity clouded his face. "Gun *me* down? Why, there's no barn-sour, town-johnny that can gun me down." Charlie's hand flashed downward in a fast draw.

The tall sight of his Remington caught in the cloth of the maroon morning coat. When Charlie jerked his arm forward, the lining tore with a loud rip. Pearly, Perk, and Davey doubled over with laughter at the sight of Charlie's ridiculous efforts and, after a moment, Charlie joined in laughing himself though he failed to see the humor in the situation. Charlie sobered first and turned to Riney, who sat against his saddle, eating from a tin plate.

"You figger we've crossed over into the U.S. of A. as yet, Riney?"

"We'll do that before noon today, Charlie. Then on to Colby."

"How far you figger it is, Riney?"

Davey Two-Knife answered instead. "Best part of a

day, maybe a day and a half." Charlie frowned with disappointment. All his efforts at getting gussied up had been wasted time. Davey took notice and added, "We ain't comin' at it the way Marv described, remember?"

Charlie gave this some thought. A weak gleam of understanding at last came to his eye. "Say, you're right there, Davey. With all that ridin' ahead of us, I suppose we oughtta get goin'. You about done prettyin' up, Pearly?"

"Since when are you bossin' this gang, Charlie?" Pearly asked rhetorically, his back turned to the others. He wiped the last of the soap from his face and rounded on Charlie, his features arranged into a haughty pose. "A man should always look his best, Charlie. There's *some* of us, though, who're beyond hope." The jibe passed over Charlie's head.

"Boys," Riney began, rising to refill his plate. "You gotta understand one thing. When we get to Colby, we have to be on our best behavior until we find out how things are run there. If we tip our hand too soon, we're liable to get a mob of townspeople down on us with lynch ropes and shotguns."

Charlie paled. "Oh, God, Riney. Don't even think about scatterguns."

"What is it about you and shotguns, Charlie?" Perk inquired mildly. "A workin' gunny like you should have been able to take that hick law dog in Montenegro easy, yet he pokes a scattergun your direction and you turn to jelly. Why?"

"Oh . . . it's . . . something happened to me a long time ago. I was only a kid. Makes no never mind, though. We do this Riney's way and we'll come out all right, right? Right?"

The rest of the gang ignored Charlie, bending to fill their mouths with beans and greasy salt pork. Affronted, Charlie took a plate from the kitchen box and helped himself to breakfast. He sat alone, casting wounded glances at his fellow outlaws and munching with a methodical, cowlike rhythm.

A bird flew over and hovered in the air above Charlie's gray beaver. Typical of its kind, the blue jay dropped a large, gray-white deposit that splattered loudly on the flat top of the tall hat, then squawked defiantly and circled its target. Charlie yelled in indignation and whipped out his revolver. He aimed at the startled jay, which flew to the protection of a nearby tree.

"Hold it, Charlie," Riney commanded. "We may need every round of ammunition when we get to Colby."

"Aw, Riney. You see what he did to me?" he asked the gang.

"Yeah," Perk replied through a guffaw. "He shit on your pretty hat. What difference does that make? It didn't cost you anything, did it?"

Charlie glowered and reholstered the Remington. He stood and walked to the small spring at the edge of their campsite. A little water, splashed on to the hat, washed away the insult, and Charlie returned to the others, who were saddling their horses.

Subdued, Charlie refrained from his ordinary constant chatter while the outlaws made ready to break camp. Not until they had ridden for a silent hour did he seem to rouse from his brooding quiet.

"Hey, Perk," Charlie began. "I remember one time

up Kansas way, in the Injun Territory it was. Had me a run-in with them Cherokee Light Horse . . . sorta policemen for the savages they are. Well, the way it was . . ."

Pearly turned in his saddle, looked back at Charlie with a black countenance that silenced the fat outlaw. "Aw, why'd you have to go and spoil it, Charlie?"

"Spoil what?"

"Our peace and quiet."

Shortly after noon on the following day, Riney Stark and his gang reined in at the top of a long, gradual slope that spread out into the broad, flat desert floor. The road they had followed for the past four hours led, arrow-straight, into the distance to where they could see the outline of haze-distorted buildings. Riney turned to his men.

"There she is, boys, Colby. You did a fine job of trail cuttin', Davey."

"Thanks, boss." Davey peered at their far-off goal. The men around him made no effort to push on. At last Charlie stirred restlessly.

"Well, sittin' here jawin' about it ain't gettin' us there. What're we doin' just hangin' around admirin' it for?"

"Charlie's right, boys. We might as well ride on in." Before he applied spurs to his mount, Riney said to the others, "Remember what I said about bein' good little boys until we find out what's what."

With a whoop, the gang jumped their horses to a gallop and thundered down the long, gradual slope, yelling louder as their prize grew clearer. At the edge of town they slowed to a walk and studied a big sign.

Paint pealed from its weathered surface, and a few bullet holes decorated its edges.

Welcome to
COLBY
A Peaceable City
Visitors Check Firearms
at Marshal's Office
Population: 250

The figure two hundred and fifty had been crossed out and several changes, each a lower number than the previous one, was daubed on in paint fresher than that of the sign. Below it, some local youngster had crudely lettered, Gettin' Smaller all the Time.

"Well, well, lookie at that." Charlie cackled. "We gonna turn in our shootin' irons, Riney?"

"All things considered, Charlie, I think that's one law we'd best not obey."

The gang moved on, looking over their surroundings. To both sides of the road they saw a few Mexican dirt farmers working on scraggly rows of corn and beans. Their loose, white peon's shirts and trousers made bright contrast to the red-orange and light brown of the ground. The *campaseños* looked up at the sound of approaching hooves, to examine the newcomers with knowing eyes.

Wise in the ways of outlaws, several of the farmers crossed themselves before returning to work. Others exchanged nervous glances, and a couple snatched the straw sombreros from their heads as a sign of submission and respect. Charlie, his childlike mind excited by this display, surged ahead of the others. He spotted a saloon sign down the block and, with a whoop of joy, he bounded into a gallop once more. The rest of the gang soon followed suit.

In a billow of red dust, Riney Stark and his gang reined in their stiff-legged mounts and flung themselves out of the saddle. They made careless tie-offs on the hitch rail and thundered across the boardwalk to the inviting bat wings of Cactus Jack's Idle Hour Saloon. Inside they were greeted by the smiling countenance of Jack McGowen, proprietor and barman.

Jack twisted one well-waxed end of his full, luxurious moustache and set aside the glass he had been polishing. "Welcome, gents. What'll you have?"

Riney and his men strode directly to the bar and spread out, eyes aglitter at the prospect of wetting down their trail-dusty throats.

"Give us five glasses and a bottle of your best whiskey," Perk ordered.

"Comin' up, gents. Looks like you rode a far piece," McGowen opined while bending to fill their needs.

"You can say that, friend," Pearly answered.

At a small table, situated in a shadowy corner of the big room, a bewhiskered, shabbily dressed rummy raised his head from the sticky, glass-ringed surface to stare bleary-eyed at the strangers. He watched them receive their whiskey and glasses and shuddered with his consuming need at the sound of the amber liquor being poured.

He sucked in his hollow, grayish cheeks. His nearly toothless mouth and thin, chapped lips, formed a remarkably funnellike appendage, a mere receptacle for the open end of a bottle. A crusted, unhealthy-looking tongue flicked out to lave the rim of that fleshly hole, and he blinked rapidly against the brightness of day. At last, decided on a course of action, he climbed to his feet and unsteadily weaved a path across the floor to the gang.

"Shay there, boys, you wouldn't be kindly disposed to make that *six* glasses, wouldja?"

Davey turned toward the sound of the voice and inspected the derelict who had shambled up to them. His lips curled in a scornful sneer, and he reached out with one hand. Davey's fingers wound into the frayed material of the man's lapels, and he lifted the boozy husk until the startled drunk's feet dangled above the floor.

"We don't share our liquor with no rum-dum barfly. So light a shuck outta here."

"That's right, ya old toss-pot," Charlie said, happy to have someone he could look down on. He dug into his vest pocket and took out a nickel. "Here's a nickel for a beer. Be happy."

Charlie tossed the nickel high in the air. Davey let go the old man's coat front, and the derelict reached eagerly for the spinning coin. A fraction of a second before his grimy fingers closed over the prize, Davey grabbed him by the back of his collar and jerked him away. The nickel hit the floor and rolled away. The drunk's face took on a greenish tinge, and his eyes filled with water while he watched closely until the nickel dropped down through a crack in the floorboards. He looked up at his tormentors in supplication, large tears rolling down his cheeks.

Davey, his voice heavy with sarcasm, spoke with mock compassion. "Aw, ain't that too bad now." He shrugged and winked at Charlie. "Well, rummy, you can always go out and grub under the buildin' for it. Just you and the spiders and the rats." He and Charlie sniggered at their cruel joke as they enjoyed the old man's misery. Then they began to toss him roughly back and forth, laughing all the while. When this new game ceased to amuse them, they started to drag the old man to the door.

"Wheew! You stink old man," Charlie yelled in the drunk's face. "You musta dirtied your drawers last night while you was all liquored up. Maybe a sluicin' off in the horse trough would make it so we could stand your company."

"Y-ya mean then . . . then you'd buy me a drink?" the rummy asked pleadingly.

"If we don't drown you first," Charlie bellowed.

Perk turned from the bar to take in the byplay and, as he took a sip from his glass of whiskey, the old man cried out excitedly. "Wait! Wait a minute. Ain't you . . . ain't you Abner Perkins?"

Perk's eyes narrowed with suspicion, though he raised a hand to stop Davey and Charlie. "What if I am?"

"You is, ain't you?" the old man continued, his voice quaking with fear, though louder. "I never forget a face. Ab Perkins from No' Ca'lina."

Perk sighed heavily, one hand straying to his gun belt. "I be."

Suddenly more confident, though still terrified, the drunk faltered. "D-don't you 'member me, Abner? Simon. Simon Coulter?"

Long buried memories flooded over Perk and brought a painful display of emotions to play across his face. He nodded slightly, and Simon continued, gaining more assurance. "I was a friend of yer mother's family, the Trasks. My boy had the place next to yourn.

Uh . . " Simon glanced apprehensively at the two toughs who held him.

"Let him go, boys," Perk rasped out tonelessly.

Davey complied at once, though Charlie retained his grasp on the old drunk. "Aw, but Perk, we's just havin' a little fun with 'im."

With a swift, threatening move, Perk stepped away from the bar and headed for Charlie. His voice held a cold, deadly tone. "I said, leave him be, Charlie."

Charlie Bell flinched, and his hand flew from Simon Coulter's shoulder. He sidestepped quickly. A smile spread on Perk's face, and he reached out a friendly hand to take Simon by the arm.

"Now, Simon, it'ud pleasure me if you join us for a small libation." He steered the blinking, astonished man to the bar and jerked his head in command. "You, mister, fetch us another glass."

"That mean I can have a drink?" Simon asked with wonder.

Startled, McGowen hesitated to comply. He had been enjoying Simon's discomfort, thinking it might be good riddance to the old lush. But the ominous power radiating from these tough gun-slicks intimidated him, and he offered a silent prayer to the Blessed Virgin that their anger might never be turned on him.

He produced another shotglass and slid it in front of Simon. Perk poured, and Simon grabbed the first drink with shaking hands, slopping half of it on the bar before he could bend his head and sip from it. He gulped it down greedily and extended the empty container for another.

"I'll . . . I'll be all right in a minute, Abner," he said in apology. "Mighty grateful to you I am, mighty grateful. Jist needs me another to . . . to make me well." Simon hastily downed the second one, then slowly sipped the refill Perk doled out for him.

"Simon, I'm right grieved at the way those two treated you," Perk said. "Why, I never recognized you till you said your name. You've changed. We all have," he added quickly to take the implied rebuke from his words. "A lot of years gone by."

"You're a real gen'leman, Abner, a real gen'leman. I thank you kindly. I heard you moved off to Geo'g'a afore the war."

"That's so, Simon. We had a right nice place there 'fore the damn Yankees came through."

"You an' your missus got a place near here now?"

A sudden dark look passed over Perk, his eyes distant, an old grief etched deeply into the lines of his face. He shook off the passing feeling and recovered his usual hard, closed expression.

"Got no more family, Simon. That damned butcher Sherman an' his men burned us out like a lot of other folks. Had me two sons, fine boys, only eight and six years growed they were. Yankees burnt them alive with the missus when she refused to leave the house . . . an' us not ownin' a single slave! Rotten Yankee bastards!" The powerful vehemence of Perk's condemnation of Sherman's men sobered Simon, who laid a compassionate hand on his friend's shoulder.

"Right sorrowful to hear that, Abner. War does powerful bad hurt to a man. Though, what can you expect from Yankees, right?" He sighed heavily. "But, what's past is past, boy. What you doin' now?" The moment he spoke, Simon regretted the question. He looked nervously from one gang member to the other while they shifted edgily under his gaze and fingered their gun belts.

"Uh . . . er . . . ah, I reckon I needn't ask that question, eh, Abner? I . . . I'll see you again 'fore you ride out, won't I? And I thank you kindly for them drinks. Best be goin' for now. Been a pleasure makin' yer acquaintance, gen'lemen." Simon nodded hesitantly to Riney and the gang and hastily departed.

The bat wing doors flopped wildly after his exit.

Amy Wilkins entered the front of the store from the back room, her arms laden with boxes of sewing thread. Ignoring the stock work she'd assigned herself, she walked directly to Howie and placed the containers on the counter. "Who are those rowdies that just rode in, Howard? I declare their awful ruckus could be heard clear in the back."

Howie looked up from his work, a vexed expression on his face. He removed a green eyeshade and shoved aside the account books. As he did, Simon Coulter slid quietly in the front door.

"How should I know, my dear? After all, I'm not the marshal around here. Don't you think these books keep me busy enough?"

Simon sidled up to the counter and licked dry lips. "I'll tell you who they are," he declared, startling Howie. "You just bet I will. Why, they's about the meanest, roughest gang of bushwhackers this territory ever produced."

Howie winced at Simon's pronouncement as he recalled all the tongue lashings his wife had given him over the barbarity of the frontier. He lifted a hopeful hand in an attempt to restrain further comment from the old drunk, who went on without pause.

"That's Riney Stark and his gang. Why, I even knows one of 'em. No' Ca'lina boy like myself." He gave Howie a "so-there" look, pleased with his own sudden self-importance.

At Simon's announcement, Amy's eyes grew large with surprise and repugnance. She turned on her husband, a finger waggling in admonition while her voice took on an accustomed lecturing tone. "Howard, you must go right now and tell Marshal Rider about this. The very idea of allowing trash like Riney Stark and that mob of killers have free run of our streets! And, mind you, Howard, if Clint Rider asks you to volunteer as a deputy, you just better do it. Do I make myself clear?"

Howie shrugged in resignation. He stood and removed his apron, then opened his mouth to form a protest, to remind her that, until recently, it had always been she who loudly denounced frontier violence and objected to drafting citizens to form a posse. He thought better of it and lay the blue-striped cloth on the counter.

"Yes, dear, I hear you." Howie turned and walked out the door, his shoulders slumped in henpecked defeat. Simon looked after him a moment, growing agitated with the excitement he had been responsible for generating. Then he turned to Amy.

"Hot dawg, Miz Wilkins. Now we're gonna see some action. Why, with Clint Rider and the son of Mason Wilkins fightin' fer the law, them owlhoots'll clear outta town in no time."

Amy's expression implied she remained somewhat

unconvinced of this cheerful prospect. She dismissed Simon and his bad news with a shrug. "Well, I certainly hope you're right, Simon. I most certainly hope so."

Chapter 11

Thick walls of mortared rock and adobe kept the low-ceilinged interior of the Colby marshal's office cool in summer and easy to warm in winter. The simple furnishings — a gun rack, scarred desk, several captain's chairs, and a squat, black wood-burning stove — had not been enlarged upon by the current occupant. The only addition Clint Rider had effected was a large nail, driven into the one side of the wooden frame, which held a tattered bulletin board. On it he hung a sheaf of wanted posters. Clint sat now, canted back in his swivel chair, listening to Howie Wilkins conclude his story.

"So you see, Clint, this could be the chance you've needed to quiet those few, but influential, people who objected to your appointment. You know what a horrid reputation Riney Stark and his gang has. Why, to be the man that—"

"You're right!" Clint snapped forward in his chair, startling his friend into silence. "It would be a feather in my cap, Howie. But you see, I have no call to arrest them."

"No call? What do you mean by that?"

"Exactly what I said, Howie. I have no warrant for their arrest. As far as I know they're not wanted for anything in New Mexico. And so far they have done nothing here to cause me to arrest them."

Confusion and apprehension spread over Howie's face and he spoke as though to himself. "Amy's not going to like this."

"*Amy* don't make the laws in Colby, or the Territory of New Mexico, Howie, and she sure as hell don't enforce them." Clint relented at his friend's pained expression. "Look, I can tell them to move on, even see Miles Parrish about a peace bond, orderin' them outta town as undesirables. As justice of the peace he can do that. Or I can send for a warrant from the nearest county that does want them. But as of this minute, I have not one single thing I can arrest Stark and the rest for."

Howie started to protest again, but the door slammed open, silencing him. Mayor Gilbert stormed into the office, agitation evident in every line of his fat body. He shook a liver-spotted fist at Clint Rider.

"Rider, what's this I hear about you allowing our fair city to become a haven for wanted criminals?"

Clint Rider's patience snapped at this, and he slammed his open palm violently on the desktop, causing small eddies of dust to rise. "Now just a damn minute, Mayor Gilbert. I figure you're talkin' about Riney Stark and his boys havin' a drink over at McGowen's Idle Time."

Gilbert puffed himself full of self-importance and indignation. "I never liked the idea of appointing you marshal. A roughrider, a gunslinger, not the sort good people want to associate with." He paused, carried away with his own rhetoric. "Just who else do you think I might be referring to, Rider?"

Clint looked cold fury at both men, who opened their mouths to add more. Clint cut them off with an angry jerk of his hand. "Rein up them flappin' jaws of yours . . . both of you." He began to rummage through his desk until he found what he sought: a wanted poster on the Stark gang from Tucson, Arizona. He held it so that each man could get a good look.

"Now here. As far as I know, this is the closest place Stark and his men are wanted. I told Howie once what I'm allowed to do by law, and I'm not wastin' time sayin' it all over again. If you want to come with me, I intend to notify the sheriff of Pinal County that they are here, and if he sends a warrant, then I can arrest them."

"And why can't you jail them first and then wire Tucson?" Mayor Gilbert blustered.

"I took this job to uphold the law," Clint reposted coldly. "Not twist it all which a way to fit the notions of any fool that could walk through that door."

Gilbert spluttered with indignation and affront. "Are . . . are you calling me a fool, Rider? The audacity." He gulped air to gain volume. "I could have your badge for that!"

Crimson fury suffused Clint Rider's face. "You *are* a fool, Gilbert. So fire me and be damned, you officious son of a bitch. Who'd handle Riney Stark for you then?"

"I, er . . . that is, I . . . ah . . ."

A brief smile quirked the corners of Clint's mouth. He cut off the mayor's mumbled confusion. "After I telegraph Tucson, I intend to go over to the Idle Time and tell Stark what I did. Then, if they want to stay and get arrested, they can. Now, are you gentlemen coming with me or, being the good sort of people, don't you want to be seen associating with me?"

Charlie Bell swallowed rapidly, downing half a mug of beer. He wiped his foam-flecked lips with the back of one hand and winked broadly at a saloon girl who had snuggled up close to him. He placed one arm around her bare shoulder and tweaked the nipple of her right breast.

"You kinda like ol' Charlie, don't ya, sweetie?" Charlie looked beyond her, his mind on the privacy of her room and the intimate pleasures she'd promised in a husky whisper only moments before. "Well then . . . uh-oh. Uh, Riney, we got company."

Riney turned in his seat at a table where a dispirited game of stud progressed and gazed toward the bat wings to see what Charlie meant. His smile broke for a moment, and then he recovered, speaking with all the oily unction of a polished politician, dropping the rough frontier idiom he affected and reverting to his normal, cultured speech.

"Well, well, marshal. I wondered how long it would take for you to get here. Come in and join the party."

Marshal Clint Rider stood in the open doorway, the swinging partitions pushed out of his way. He wore the same clothes he usually affected for his job: black trousers, vest, coat and hat, a snowy linen shirt, and dark string tie to complete the ensemble. He rested one hand lightly on the butt of his Colt Frontier, the other he used to carelessly tip back the brim of his Stetson. He spoke in a calm, even tone:

"You might have known I'd be here soon enough."

"Oh, I most assuredly did. To what do we owe the honor of your presence?"

"Mr. Stark, I got no warrant for you or your gang, got no idea of takin' you in. I only came to give you a warning."

Riney's eyes narrowed dangerously, an angry fire glittering within. "Not many men get away with that, marshal."

"Call it friendly advice, then. I only want you to know how it is. I sent a telegram to Tucson. If the sheriff there sends me a warrant, I'll have to come after you. Figure that will take until tomorrow mornin', so you got that long to make up your mind."

Riney's reply came as a low, ominous growl. "That's inhospitable at best, marshal. Your precipitous action has bought you a bullet. No man's ever come after me like that and lived."

Clint ignored the menace and addressed himself to the rest of the gang. "You men are welcome to stay here and drink, have a good time, so long as you mind your ways. Then you can ride out of here, and nobody gets harmed. But if I get that warrant from Tucson and you're still in town, I'll jail the lot of you. So, you see, it would be best for you—"

Davey Two-Knife stepped quietly from the bar, menace in his posture, his hand hovering over his sixgun. His words, in an angry tone, mocked the marshal. " 'It would be best for you . . .' to just go off fishin' for a while, marshal. You get in our way, we'll put the sod over you."

Clint quirked a half smile that seemed a bit sad, and his reply came in a slow, measured beat. "You don't frighten me, Davey Two-Knife. You never did. When you were a little boy I turned you over my knee and spanked your butt . . . after I bloodied your nose." He took a deep breath, expelled it in a gust. "I'm Clint Rider."

"Clint! Clint Rider?" Davey's face beamed with happiness, and he rushed toward the lawman, arms spread wide. "Clint!" Davey embraced the unmoving marshal, then stepped back a pace, still holding Clint by both shoulders. "You ever tell anyone else you whopped me and I'll make a liar outta you. If you weren't ten pounds heavier and three years older than me, you'd never done it nohow." He extended his hand for Clint to shake.

Clint looked at Davey's hand with an expression that implied the appendage had come from the bottom of an outhouse and refused to clasp it. Hurt, Davey tried to hide the embarrassment it caused him in front of his friends. He slapped Clint on the shoulder and urged his childhood friend toward the bar.

"Have a drink with me, Clint. For old-time's sake, huh?"

Clint smiled a bit sadly, then shook his head. "I won't shake your hand, Davey, and I won't drink with you. We're from two different worlds now. Why, I'll never know. You'd have made a damn fine lawman, Davey."

The half-breed tried a bluff laugh that failed. "Me? A law dog? You know how much I hated bein' made to do things."

A gulf of sorrow filled Clint's eyes. "I know. Forever the rebel, Davey. Maybe that's why I always thought of you as my best friend. I . . . well, I guess I sorta looked up to you as some kind of hero."

Nonplussed, Davey could only stammer his reply. "Gee, damn, Clint, I . . . well, I mean . . ." He brightened. "But . . ."

"But those days are gone. There was a wild streak in you then, Davey. What's happened to it now?"

Suddenly on the defensive and deeply torn emotionally by this unexpected reunion with the only person he'd ever loved or respected, Davey felt compelled to explain himself. "Clint, you recollect I was ten before I knew I was even part white. And I only lived with your kind for three years. After Maw died, I went back to the Comanches."

"At fourteen, as I remember. That'd make it four years. What have you done with yourself since then?"

"Well, you know I never saw myself as all that white. I rode with old Stand Wate and his Cherokee for the Confederacy. Hear you wore the gray, too. Killed you a bunch of Yankees, I'll bet."

"Yes, I was with Hood's Texans. But after the war I put that kind of killing behind me." Clint sighed heavily. "How many men have you killed since?"

Davey started to answer, but Riney interrupted, his mouth twisted into an indolent sneer. "Your reunion is touching, gentlemen, but it's time to end it." He turned hotly angry eyes on Clint Rider. "Marshal, you came here to tell us to drink up and get out of town or you'd jail us. That you've done. Now I'll have a turn at handin' out information. Listen well, because I'm only saying it once.

"The hick-town lawman hasn't been born yet who can lock us in any jail. We like this town and intend to stay some while. If you do get a warrant for our arrest, I would advise you to bury it somewhere in your desk and forget all about us. There's five of us." His voice reverted to the crude slang of the West. "The meanest, baddest bunch you ever saw. You got any ideas of sittin' and tellin' your grandkids that you knew the awful outlaw, Davey Two-Knife, just best forget that high-handed talk about our goin' behind bars."

Davey tried to intervene, his loyalties torn between the gang and his friend. "Clint won't give us no trouble now, boss. Not with me here."

A sad, but knowing, smile crossed Riney's lips. "That's where you're wrong, Davey. Precisely because you're here, he will have to. There's no way I know of to shy away from what needs doing and still remain a man in your own eyes."

Clint nodded acknowledgement. "You sound like a thoughtful, educated man, Mr. Stark. What a waste to have chosen the life you're living." He turned his remarks to Davey.

"Davey, your boss, Riney, is right. If I get that paper, I will come after you. I couldn't look myself in the face again if I didn't. Now, old friend . . . and you, too, gentlemen, drink up. To avoid any unpleasantness I would advise you to be out of town by sunup."

Without waiting for a reply, Clint turned and walked away. When he reached the swinging doors he stopped momentarily and looked at Davey, all the sorrow and bitter loss of crumbling hero worship evident on his face. He started to speak, then caught himself. One hand unconsciously made a gesture of appeal, then he nodded curtly to them all and walked out.

Behind him, Charlie Bell let out a long, tensely held breath in a whistling sigh. "Whewee! Well, I'll be dogged. Davey, why didn't you tell us you knew the lawman in this town?"

"I didn't know . . . least till he came in here."

"You seem to be mighty chummy like," Perk inserted, eyes glimmering with suspicion.

Davey seemed unaffected by it. "Ought to. When my maw left the Comanche and went back to her own people we lived with Clint's folks. Seems as how they was some sort of shirttail relation. An' nobody else would have us. It weren't a good life in those years. The other kids in town used to call me names and throw rocks, but not Clint. No, sir, not Clint.

"Do we know each other? I reckon so. We's brothers . . . least ways blood brothers. Clint wasn't ashamed of havin' us live with them. The good people of town called me an unclean little heathen savage, but Clint would spit at 'em, an' one Sunday he even put some nice soft, fresh meadow muffins in their pews at church. Lordy did that ever make a stink." The gang laughed at Davey's unintentional pun. The hardened outlaw had taken on a gentle, distant look, happy memories flooding over him.

"Clint an' me slept in the same room. He said it would make him a braver man livin' close to an Indian. Just one time we ever fought . . . just once. And that was over a girl." He sighed heavily.

"Here, what you need is a drink." Riney shoved a glass over in front of Davey's hand.

"Uh . . . yeah, I do need a little. But Riney, promise me one thing, will you?"

"What's that?"

Tears welled in Davey's eyes, and he brushed angrily at them to keep the moisture from falling. "If . . . if it ever comes to a showdown, an' we gotta go against

Clint, promise me that . . . that I don't have to do it. Don't make me gun him down. Will you do that?"

Riney looked uncomfortable and not a little embarrassed, not so much for himself but for Davey. He cleared his throat in the midst of a prolonged silence while the others looked on in a state of stupefied awe. He hacked and spat and refilled Davey's glass.

"Sure, kid, sure. Now drink up. Drink up."

Davey smiled nervously, shyly, took the proferred glass and downed a stiff double shot in a swallow. He extended the empty for another and shook his head in gratitude.

Chapter 12

Five men occupied the captain's chairs in Clint Rider's office: Mayor Gilbert and the four city councilmen of Colby. Their faces wore expressions of indignation.

Clint, on the other hand, appeared grim though determined. Yellow light illuminated the room from the twin wicks of hanging kerosene lamps. Outside darkness filled the streets of Colby, and from the distant Idle Time Saloon came the sounds of a tinkling piano, the shrill, professional laughter of the "working girls," and the frequent shouts of raucous pleasure from the members of Riney Stark's gang and the few stray cowhands giving Jack McGowen their custom.

"Gentlemen, it appears the problem is a great deal more difficult than I had anticipated. I have not as yet received a reply from Tucson. Didn't expect any until tomorrow morning, in fact."

"Which leaves our fair city at the mercy of those . . . desperados," Mayor Gilbert snapped testily.

"No, Mr. Mayor," Clint contradicted with a weary sigh. "What it does is leave our town with the possibility of a bloody confrontation if it becomes necessary to try to arrest Riney Stark and his men."

"*Try* to arrest, marshal?" Abe Goldman, the gunsmith, diamond, and watch dealer in Colby asked shrewdly.

"Abe, I shouldn't have to remind you that there are five of them. Five professional guns. I have two deputies. I might, if the situation arises, be able to count on Howie Wilkins."

Mayor Gilbert beamed expansively. He had led a faction in town that had tried to get Howie to accept the position of marshal. He believed absolutely in the hereditary inheritance of such attributes as fortitude, courage, and skill in gun handling. He had been bitterly disappointed at Howie's refusal. Though, it appeared, no amount of exposure to reality could shake his conviction.

"Well, Rider, with the son of Mason Wilkins backing you, you shouldn't have any trouble at all."

Clint ran a hand through the thick shock of his hair and let his shoulders slump in resignation. "Mayor Gilbert, much as I like Howie, he is not his father. Under most circumstances, he wouldn't say boo to a goose. The sooner you come to terms with that fact, the better off we'll be in this discussion."

"Are you contradicting me?" Gilbert pompously demanded.

For a moment, Clint's temper flared. "Hell, yes, I'm contradicting you, Mr. Mayor! Let me repeat the facts, since they apparently have failed to impress you.

"First we have Riney Stark, who is wanted for who knows how many murders, bank, and stage robberies. Next," Clint said, ticking off the elements of his argument by folding down the fingers of one hand. "We have George Thurmon Wilson, known as Pearly. A quiet, deadly killer, wanted for seven deliberate murders and the victor of Lord knows how many 'fair' gunfights. After that, Abner Perkins, one of those for whom the War Between the States was never over. Tucson alone wants him for three killings involved in a bank robbery by the gang. Then there's Davey Two-Knife, a half-breed who lived his first ten years among the Comanche and went back to them before his fifteenth birthday. He thinks like an Indian and kills just as casually as one. Last . . ." Clint shook his head as though to ward off unpleasant images. "Last there's Charlie Bell. A mad-dog killer with the mind of a ten-year-old. They say he still likes to pull apart frogs and tear the wings from flies, one of the gentler habits he picked up in childhood. He back-shot his first man at the age of eleven and is supposed to have giggled while he mutilated the victim's privates.

"There isn't a one of them that can't take a Winchester and hit a target at two hundred yards from horseback. With a handgun any of them can make everyone else look like rank amateurs. Now, they just happen to come to Colby, and you expect one man to face them down."

Four faces glared at Clint in self-righteous indignation. Only Miles Parrish, the city magistrate, had the good grace to look sheepish.

"Oh, I'd have men to back me, all right," Clint hastened to add to stave off an objection from Mayor Gilbert. "A farm boy, hardly dry behind the ears, who has been a deputy for only a little over a year. And a middle-aged, soft-belly, part-time drunk. I'm not complaining, gentlemen, they're all I have . . . all I could get for the wages you were willing to pay.

"They're fine at what they do: shakin' doorknobs, draggin' buck-naked little boys outta the creek and sendin' them back to school; coolin' off rowdy cowhands hoorawin' the town. But the Riney Stark gang ain't made up of cowpunchers drunk on a month's pay and lettin' off steam. They're killers, gentlemen, in case you've forgotten.

"Now, what I'd like to know is this. How many of you will be out there with me?"

"Why, er . . . ah . . . that is . . ." Mayor Gilbert began to bluster, deflated of his earlier pomposity. "It's *your* job, Rider. We hired you to be marshal. It's not our place to—"

"Might be he has another reason for not wantin' to arrest 'em, Bryce," Jim Tyson, the banker, sneered, addressing the mayor. "Way I hear it, him an' that Davey Two-Knife grew up together. Like brothers they was. Could be he don't want to put his friend behind bars."

"You son of a bitch!" Clint exploded. He leaped to his feet and bent far over his desk, pushed his face close to the suddenly pale, thoroughly intimidated banker. For a second their eyes locked, then, with trembling lip, Jim Tyson glanced away.

"You sit down there in that bank of yours, behind stacks of money and determine the success or ruin of everyone for twenty miles around, usin' an ink pen and ledger book to torment 'em like a witch uses pins. Then when it comes to a real showdown, you ain't got balls enough to stand up and be counted. No, all you can do is sit there and spew out insinuations from that nasty little mind of yours."

Mayor Gilbert rose and tried to insert himself between the angry marshal and frightened banker. "Gentlemen, gentlemen, let's not quarrel among ourselves. We're facing a crisis. Marshal Rider has convinced me of that. Let our little differences lie. What is it you want from us, ah, er, Clint?" He tried a political smile of pseudo-sincerity.

"I want guns and the men to use them. For openers, how about Ed Parker down at the bank?"

"Out of the question!" Tyson snapped. "I need him there to protect the bank from those outlaws."

"You're stupid as well as yellow, aren't you, Tyson?" Clint taunted. "If we don't have enough men to arrest Stark and his gang in the morning, just how the hell much good do you think Ed will do you all alone down at the bank?"

"All right, all right," Tyson whined. "I'll see that he reports to you first thing in the morning."

"Who else?" Clint demanded.

"How about Bart Quiller? He don't work tomorrow's stage run," Abe Goldman suggested.

"Good. Any others you can name?"

"You can count on me," Miles Parrish said quietly. "That Greener of mine'll make 'em sit up and take notice."

Clint felt a warm glow of gratitude spread through his chest. "No, Miles. I'll need you to hold a hearing and sign the order to keep Stark and the others in jail until someone gets here from Tucson. I appreciate the offer, though. Any more ideas?"

"You'd mentioned Howard Wilkins," Mayor Gilbert supplied.

"Forget Howie. He wouldn't have the chance of a fart

in a windstorm against Stark's bunch. Can you think of a single other soul?"

"Well . . . right off hand . . ." Mayor Gilbert began hesitantly.

"We can't rightly . . ." Jim Tyson added, lapsing off into silence.

"What we mean is, we can't think of anyone else," Abe Goldman concluded. From the corner, where he'd sat during the entire discussion, Miles Parrish merely shook his head in negative support of the others' opinion.

"Dandy, just dandy. Five men. A bank guard, a shotgun rider on the stage line, two inexperienced deputies, and me. At least it gives us equal numbers. If we can do it by surprise, we might have a chance."

"Then you'll go ahead with arresting them?" Mayor Gilbert asked brightly.

"If the warrant comes."

"What do you mean by that?" the major demanded indignantly, his former arrogance returned by the resolution of the problem.

"No warrant, no arrest."

"I told you so," Jim Tyson purred nastily. "These gun-slicks are all alike. Figures he'd side with his friend."

"Now, Jim . . ." Mayor Gilbert began, seeking to avoid another violent outbreak.

Clint Rider bristled. His face clouded with black anger, and he stalked from behind his desk, his tread heavy and menacing. He reached out with both hands and wound them into Jim Tyson's lapels. With a soft grunt of effort, he jerked the portly banker off his chair and held him, dangling, in the air.

"I'll say this once and only once. If the job came to me to do, I'd hang Davey Two-Knife or any of the others. I signed on to uphold the law in Colby. I do it my way, and I don't tailor the law to suit the whims of fat-gut cowards like you, Tyson. Keep your foul mouth shut and stay out of my sight or I'll beat you black-eyed and bloody. After this affair with Stark is over, I don't give a damn what you do with the job of marshal. For all I care you can take this badge and stuff it up your—"

"Please!" Mayor Gilbert interrupted. "Now's not the time for personalities. We can discuss all that after Stark is dealt with. Please, gentlemen?"

"Aw, let Clint punch him one, Bryce," Miles Parrish suggested, a happy smile on his face. "Jim's got it coming."

Clint released his hold on the banker, who slumped gratefully into his chair. "All right, Mr. Mayor. Tomorrow morning decides what we'll do."

Natana-jo lay on the ground beneath the stars. He had been like this most of the night, troubled thoughts keeping sleep from him. Soon the red ball of the sun, mighty symbol of the Great Spirit, would return in the east and bring day back to the eyes of man. Yet he had no answer, certainly not a simple one to what faced them.

All the signs indicated that the *Pen-dik-olye* demons they pursued had ridden down into the white-eyes' village. How long would they stay? Would it mean more bloodshed, more killing of their own kind? With each death scream, the spirit of the dying man was given up to strengthen the power of the demon who did the slaying. In a place of so many white-eye lodges, would they not become too strong to kill? That place of the white devils, the one the white-eyes called Colby, lay two suns' ride away. Should they go there or wait for the bad ones to come to them for vengeance? Had they not already revenged themselves against the *Me-ji-kanos* who bought their families' scalps?

That question had been asked by several of his warriors. They had also pointed out that they had guns and bullets to trade with their Apache brothers. And the shiny white metal so prized by the white renegades with whom they often bargained. What to do? What to do, he wondered. The sound of a soft footstep reached *Natana-jo's* ears and he half rose, knife in hand, instantly alert.

Satanta knelt beside his war chief and closest friend. "You do not seek your peace in dreams, my brother."

"No. I cannot. There are many things to think on."

"We must go on. We must kill them all." Satanta's voice quavered with the intensity of his appeal. "We have to kill all the *Pen-dik-olye* in that village. They give food, shelter, and comfort to those we seek. That makes them equally bad."

Suddenly *Natana-jo's* mind cleared, his decision made. "No. That we cannot do. This is not Apache land. We are far beyond the homes of the Mescaleros, the Mimbranos. Even the land of the White Mountain people lies many suns' ride behind us. We have no quarrel with these white-eyes. As we have seen before, the demons we hunt spread death and destruction among their own kind. Whatever the evil ones receive in the village, old friend, rest assured they do not get freely. Go now and rest. In the morning we will hold counsel and decide."

Early morning light found nothing outwardly changed in Colby. The usual routine went on with monotonous regularity. Those who could afford it or had no means of fixing their own breakfast had filled the cafe, including the Riney Stark gang. Charlie Bell finished first, gulping his food down like a starved dog. Perk Perkins and Pearly Wilson pushed back their plates a few minutes later. All three rose from their chairs and strolled out into the weak sunshine.

Charlie worked elaborately on his teeth with a wooden toothpick. Two overdressed dowagers, hurrying to the same destination the gang members had vacated, came bustling along the boardwalk toward them. Perk and Pearly stepped politely aside to allow them room to pass, Pearly tipping his hat with a flourish. The two well-padded females talked with animated agitation, making sure their words carried to all ears nearby.

"And can you believe it, Mildred," one remarked to the other in her most silken, catty tone. "There they are, the five of them, holding up in that evil saloon, drinking, gambling and all sorts of immoral things. Why doesn't our fine marshal do something about this, I wonder?"

Not one to leave her own claws unsheathed, Mildred purred back, "Well, my dear Cora, your husband *is* the mayor. Why don't you make him put pressure on Mr. Rider to do something? I agree, it is most disgraceful the way those outlaws are allowed to have their run of our fine town. Shameful."

They had progressed beyond the three outlaws now and neared the front of the cafe. Riney Stark stepped through the doorway and held it open for them, tipping his hat. He smiled at the nature of their conversation and put on a droll face.

"Oh, I agree with you, ma'am. Yes siree. I think it is a shame and a disgrace the way the marshal coddles those murderers. The very idea of allowing men like that to sit around perfectly free to drink and carouse with painted women. Something must be done."

"Wha . . . why, thank you, young man," the mayor's wife responded, taken aback by this unexpected source of support. Despite her consternation, she quickly rose to the occasion with the consummate ease of a politician's wife. "It's not often that one finds such uplifting sentiments among the men of our community. If only we had more like you, our temperance movement would flourish. Or, perhaps if you were our marshal, something could be done," she added thoughtfully. "Are you new here? I don't believe I recall your face."

"Oh, yes, ma'am. This is my first trip to Colby. What a shame to have it spoiled by such as the goin's on in the saloon."

Cora Gilbert turned a triumphant face on her companion, Mildred Tyson, eager to drive home her new-gained advantage. "You see, Mildred. At least we have the support of *some* of the men in town. From what I hear, *your* husband wouldn't do anything and even begrudged Marshal Rider the use of Ed Parker for a deputy."

She looked smugly back at Riney, not noticing that the gang members had slipped quietly back to where they could hear the conversation and now stood grinning with high good humor. "I certainly thank you for your opinion on this matter, Mister . . . uh, I don't believe we heard your name?"

Riney smiled broadly, his eyes twinkling with mischief as he swept his hat from his head and made a low, mocking bow. "Stark, ma'am. Riney Stark."

Riney's words washed over the hefty dowagers like a bucket of cold water. They blinked their eyes, gaped in shock and horror. "Riney Stark?" the mayor's wife gabbled breathlessly.

"Riney Stark the outlaw?" Mildred Tyson squealed in horror.

They gathered their skirts and rushed off down the street emitting gasps of amazement and fear. Behind them a chorus of vulgar laughter followed. Charlie detached himself from the others and galloped along in the fleeing matrons' wake, yapping like a small dog. His antics only served to increase the women's hurried, undignified flight.

When their coarse laughter finally died down, Pearly looked to Riney. "When do we take over this place, boss?"

Riney glanced about the empty early morning streets and twisted his lips into a wicked smile. "We start right now. Let's head for the saloon and lay out plans."

Quickly they walked down two doors and entered the Idle Time through the bat wings. Inside, Jack McGowen worked behind the bar, polishing and stacking glasses from the previous night's business. He looked up when he heard the gang enter, then paled at the sight of their drawn guns. McGowen ducked below the counter when Perk and Charlie fired several shots into the ceiling.

Three saloon girls stood near the piano, going over the words to a song the young player pounded out slowly so they could learn the tune. When Perk's Remington crashed to life, the ladies of the evening shrieked in terror and dived below the roulette table to find shelter. The piano artist collapsed limply across the keys, and a large, wet stain spread at his crotch. He felt the slowly creeping moisture and revived enough to cry in terror.

"Oh, my God, I'm shot!"

"Naw, Sissy Boy," Charlie informed him, advancing on the hapless musician. "You jist peed yourself." He turned back to the bar when McGowen's head appeared above the polished surface. "Set up a bottle and five glasses, boy. You're workin' for us now."

"Wha . . . what do you mean?" McGowen asked in a plaintive whine, only too sure what the fat outlaw meant.

"We've taken a likin' to this place. Decided to make it our town. Any objections?"

"Na-no," McGowen stammered, visions of his life's efforts going down the drain in the drunken excesses of these crazed gunmen. His hand trembled so badly the glasses clinked musically together when he brought them from the back bar. He nearly dropped the whiskey trying to uncork the bottle, which he sat down with a jerky, uncoordinated motion. Then he ducked behind the counter again as Perk swung his gun past McGowen's middle in an arc that encompassed a quarter of the room.

Perk blasted a shot into the wall a fraction of an inch

above the piano player's head. The frightened young man had been trying to silently sneak out of the saloon. "No you don't, boy. We figger on havin' us a good time. Best git to ticklin' those ivories."

The pianist's delicate, girlish face puckered as though he might cry and he wrung long, sensitive fingers. Then with a gasp, he darted to his instrument and plopped onto the bench. Disjointed, tuneless chords tumbled from the sound box as the quaking musician hastened to comply. From under the roulette table the girls continued to shout for mercy. Charlie looked at them and began to giggle insanely. He walked toward the three soiled doves, their faces pale under the over-painted facade of their profession. One hand groped the burgeoning swelling in Charlie's crotch.

Four men stood expectantly around Clint Rider's desk, their heads jerking violently toward the street at the sound of shots being fired in the Idle Time Saloon. Clint entered the room, his face buried behind the yellow pulp form of a telegraph message. He waved it at the others.

"Here it is, men. We have a warrant from Tucson. Now we gotta do our duty and serve it. We must take them fast and by surprise. Billy, you an' Bart circle and go through the alley, come in the back door of the Idle Time. Us three will take 'em from the front."

Billy Ash nodded solemnly and stepped to the door with Bart Quiller. Bart, a short barrel of a man, with broad shoulders and a bulldog face, looked like he could handle all the meanness anyone cared to hand out. Another shot boomed dully from the saloon.

"Looks like they're up to some meanness bright and early," Ed Parker said.

"More the reason why we have to be careful. They wouldn't be doin' that and not expect us to come runnin'. Let's go." Clint Rider tugged the brim of his Stetson down hard on his forehead and led the way out of his office.

Once in the street, the marshal and his deputies spread out and walked with grim determination to the corner, where Clint, Ed Parker, and Matt Dolan, his other full-time deputy, broke off to advance along the main drag. Billy Ash and Bart Quiller continued along to the alleyway.

An ominous silence came over the streets of Colby while the men moved into their selected positions.

Howie Wilkins worked on the outside displays arranged on the boardwalk in front of his store. He stopped when he saw his friend approaching with the other men, Winchesters slung loosely in the crook of their right arms. In an instant he realized what their objective would be. He scurried inside, closed and locked the door and drew the green shades. Clint marched on, unmindful of his friend's frightened retreat. He stopped two doors down from the saloon and drew his huge turnip watch from a vest pocket.

"We'll give 'em a minute more to get into place behind the saloon. Then we call for Stark's surrender."

Perk Perkins stood near one of the large gilt-edged windows at the front of the Idle Time Saloon. He draped one arm around the bare shoulders of a saloon girl, fingers idly teasing the swelling nipple of one breast. He glanced casually through the glass and stiffened at the scene in the middle of the street.

"Davey, looks like your marshal friend's back. Only this time he don't look so friendly."

Davey pushed away from the bar. "Let me go talk with him."

Riney reached out a restraining hand, holding Davey by one arm. "No, Davey. It's too late now for talk."

"That's right," Perk added, pushing the girl away from him. "He's got two friends with him."

The whole gang froze at the sound of Clint's voice, loud in the silence from the street. "Stark! Riney Stark! You and your men come out with your hands up. I have a warrant for your arrest here, signed by the sheriff of Pinal County, Arizona Territory. Give up and there won't be any trouble."

Chapter 13

"You know what you can do with it, marshal," Perk growled. He broke out a small, decorative pane of glass beside the larger square of the front window.

"Yeah." Charlie Bell giggled. "Stuff that warrant where the sun don't shine, marshal."

"I promise you'll get a fair trial."

"How, marshal? In Tucson? Don't make me laugh." Riney's voice changed tone, tenseness evident as he checked his gun, loosening it in the holster. "We got our own style of fair trial, marshal. We're comin' out."

Davey's hurt and anguish played across his face, warring with his loyalty to the gang. "No, Riney. Please, no!"

A note of regret, almost of sadness, crept into Riney's voice. "It would be foolish of me to tell you the choices, pard. You already know them."

The remainder of the gang walked toward the door while Davey hesitated near the bar. For a second his eyes swam with tears, which he angrily brushed away before they could be shed. He breathed deeply, gusting the air out of his lungs in a prolonged sigh. Hand on the well-worn grips of his Colt's Dragoon, he stalked to the bat wings, shouldering through beside Pearly.

Outside, Riney, Perk, and Charlie stood in the street, facing Clint Rider with some ten feet separating the contending factions. For a moment, Davey looked upon the scene like something from an otherworldly drama. A vague hope rose in him that the killing could still be avoided. Riney's voice sounded distant and enormously sad.

"I told you, marshal, forget that warrant."

"I took an oath to uphold the law, Stark. You're a gentleman, you know I gotta live up to it."

Riney bowed slightly in acknowledgement and, it seemed, under the burden of his regret. "I'm sorry, then, marshal. For Davey, too. I'm real sorry."

Clint threw the Winchester to his shoulder and fired off a round. But the outlaws had moved even faster.

Riney whipped out his Colt Navy with blurring speed, eared back the hammer and took slow, careful aim. Clint's first bullet punched a hole through Charlie's fancy maroon coat and whistled harmlessly off down the street. Clint worked the lever rapidly while the hammer contacted the percussion cap on Riney's first load.

The slug caught Clint in the leg, knocked him partway around and caused him to sprawl in the dirt. The two deputies, caught a bit off guard, were slow to react. Perk and Charlie's revolvers blasted as one, the bullets tearing into flesh on each of the two lawmen. Mat Dolan doubled over from the force of the smashing blow to his abdomen, dropped his rifle and abruptly sat down in the middle of the street. His hands covered a seeping wound that quickly stained his white shirt crimson. After a second, he began to moan.

Ed Parker had been in the process of a sidestep when Perk's .44 slug smashed into his upper arm, shattering the humerus and ripping muscle tissue out the inside of his left arm before puncturing his chest cavity and expending its energy in exploding a lung. He dropped without a sound.

Riney eared back the hammer and fired again.

Nothing happened.

He quickly cocked the weapon a third time and experienced another misfire. Clint sat upright and drew his own sixgun. He snapped off a shot that plowed up dirt between Riney's legs, cranked back the hammer and took better aim.

Pearly had his own piece in play by then, discharging a round that smacked meatily into Clint's right shoulder. The impact knocked the already weakened marshal back onto the ground.

Perk and Charlie pumped bullet after bullet into the fallen deputies, the slow-witted Charlie cackling with macabre glee as dust, cloth, and blood flew from their riddled victims. Meanwhile, Riney's revolver continued to misfire. He jammed it back in the holster and drew his second sixgun, taking slow, careful aim at Clint Rider.

Clint tried to rise again, Remington in his left hand now. He made it to a sitting position when Riney squeezed the trigger of his second weapon.

A 140 grain .36 caliber round ball smashed into Clint's chest, puncturing his heart and driving the doomed lawman back with enough force that his legs and feet flopped violently before his head hit the ground. Riney fired again and yet a third time, one bullet blasting a dime-sized hole in the top of Clint's head.

Davey, who had not even drawn, cried out from the porch, his words choked with emotion, tears streaming down his face. "For God's sake, Riney, he's dead!"

Sudden quiet enveloped the main street of Colby. For a moment, no one moved. Charlie, at last, came out of his crouch and began to advance toward the fallen peace officers, his mouth dribbling spittle and a wild, glazed look in his eyes.

Riney let out a long, heavy sigh and Perk began to reload.

"Throw up your hands!" Unseen by the gang, the other two deputies had entered the saloon and crept quietly to the door. Billy Ash led the way, shouting his command as he surged onto the porch.

At the sound of Billy's voice, Davey and Pearly, who stood nearest to the entrance, turned sideways, facing each other. Their sixguns moved with lightning speed, centering on the young deputy. Shots crashed out, one on top of the other, the big .44 and .45 slugs shredding intestines and pulping Billy's organs with devastating force. He seemed to swell a moment, then pitched onto the boardwalk, a great gout of blackish blood vomiting from his mouth. Bart Quiller, a step behind Billy, burst onto the scene totally unprepared for the slaughter.

Pearly shot Bart through the eye. Bart's shotgun blasted a hole in the flooring of the overhanging balcony, and he tottered forward another pace before being slammed by three bullets fired from the street. Riney, Perk, and Charlie each put a slug into the already dead deputy's chest, only a fraction of a second part. The tremendous impact sent Bart smashing through the bat wings to crash loudly onto the sawdust-strewn floor.

Pearly and Charlie entered and dragged the corpse outside to pile with the rest, like gruesome cordwood. Davey wandered apart from the others, crossed to where Clint lay and knelt beside his friend of bygone days. Large tears coursed down his bronze cheeks. Softly, under his breath, he began to chant the Comanche death song.

"Best be gettin' an undertaker," Charlie offered helpfully. He bent and rifled the pockets of one dead deputy. For his efforts he received a handful of small change. "Better hurry. These bodies'll set up a powerful stink when the sun is full up."

Davey smoothed the blood-matted hair away from Clint's forehead and placed the marshal's hat over the dead, staring eyes. "I'll tend to that," he volunteered in a quiet tone, voice thick with grief.

Once more Davey glanced down at his friend, the last contact with decency he had. He bent forward, his body rocking in misery, wracked by tearing sobs for which he felt no shame.

Miles Parrish, justice of the peace, undertaker, and dealer in furniture and heirlooms, looked up from his coffee and copy of the *Mortician's Journal* at the sound of slow, heavily laden footsteps approaching his office. He had heard the gunshots earlier and, since several minutes had passed with no one coming to summon him, he assumed his services were not needed. Apparently Clint had been lucky, though he felt regret at not having been along to effect the arrest. His full, colorless lips twisted into a moue of distaste, distorting the luxurious moustache that grew above them, when the figure of a squat, bowlegged man appeared in his doorway, carrying in his arms a dirt-begrimed and blood-splattered corpse.

"It's customary for this establishment to pick up its . . . ah, clients, sir. There's no need to deliver them."

"It's . . . it's the marshal. He's been shot. Where should I put him?"

Miles paled at mention of Clint's death. "Then he . . . it's . . . The outlaws at the Idle Time did this?"

Shame drove Davey's eyes from those of the shocked mortician. "Yes. I . . . I want Clint to have the best funeral you can do up. No expense too great."

"Of course, of course. Everything will be taken care of. Who are you, may I ask?"

"I'm his friend. I . . . I loved him as a brother."

"Your name, sir? Your name? For the records, you understand."

"Davey Two-Knife."

"D-Davey . . . Two . . . Knife?" The mortician's eyes bugged, and his skin grew clammy, cold, damp sweat breaking out. Then suddenly rage swept away his momentary fear. "Then you're one of those bastards. You're custom is not welcome here. Get the hell out of my office."

"But . . . Clint was my friend. I want him to have a

decent burial. Please." The look of misery and contrition on Davey's face shocked Miles out of his anger.

"I . . . think I understand. It goes without saying that the town would honor a brave man. In light of your . . . ah, obvious grief, your wishes will be taken into consideration."

"Thank you." Davey tenderly laid Clint's body on the carpet in front of Miles's desk and started from the room. "There's a bunch more dead ones outside the Idle Time, undertaker. Best be goin' after them." He recovered his former toughness with a growl deep in his throat. "But I'm payin' for Clint, you hear? I'm payin' and it had better be good."

Miles Parrish trembled with renewed fury after Davey left his office. With Clint Rider dead, how could they face down these outlaws?

"All right, boys. Here's how we work this. Perk, you take the bank and the gunsmith and that harness maker's place. Pearly, go across the street and hit that general mercantile, the ladies' millinery store, and the stage-line office. We'll probably have to post someone there to keep them from slipping word out about our takeover, but for now just bust up the telegraph key.

"Charlie, you visit the blacksmith, the livery, and the feed and grain dealer," Riney concluded.

"Ain't you gonna do any work, Riney?" Charlie complained from his chair at a table near the bat wing doors of the Idle Time Saloon.

"Of course I am, Charlie. I'm going to pay a call on the cafe, the marshal's office, the other saloon, the undertaking parlor, and Mae Hennings' fancy bordello."

"You have all the luck, Riney," Perk growled. "What about the churches?"

Momentary surprise crossed Riney's face. "Good idea, Perk. No reason they shouldn't donate as well."

"What do you have for Davey to do when he gets back?" Pearly inquired.

"I think we'll let him sit this one out a while. By the way, Perk, come by the marshal's office when you get done. We'll gather up all the arms. Wouldn't do to have too many guns floatin' around town while we're lootin' all these nice folks."

"Sure, boss. A feller don't have a gun, he can't fight back." Perk drew himself erect and ambled out the door into the street. Drying blood still darkly stained the red-orange soil, and he noticed a somber-looking, glass-sided coach, drawn by a pair of dapple grays standing in the middle of Main Street. Two men worked industriously to load the bodies inside.

"Mornin', ma'am," Pearly Wilson purred like a mouse-stuffed tomcat and directed a toothy white smile toward Amy Wilkins. "I represent the Colby Businessmen's Protective League. Starting today, we will be collecting twenty-five percent of each day's receipts in order to insure you are not bothered by Riney Stark and his gang."

Anger flared in Amy's eyes, and she placed her small fists on her hips. "Get out of here, you filthy animal! You're one of them. I know you are. You'll get nothing from us, nothing! Do you understand?"

"Yes, I do, ma'am. But it appears you don't. Surely you wouldn't want those nice, expensive glass windows broken, would you?" He hefted a sad iron from the counter display, spun on one heel and hurled it through a broad front window.

Glass shattered with a musical tinkle, and Amy covered her face with both hands to stifle a sob. Pearly faced back toward her. "Or perhaps coal oil poured all over your merchandise? Or maybe a fire started by rowdies? You see, the Protective League will undertake to prevent such unpleasantness. Those who join and contribute will be protected; those who don't . . . won't. A simple, straightforward business proposition."

"Extortion, you mean. You must be out of your minds." Amy seized a broom and swung it at Pearly, knocking off his low-crowned, light tan hat. "Get out of this store, you hear me? Get out of here!"

All over town the same scene was acted out with only slight variations. Most of the town's businessmen paid out of fear. Only at the bank did Perk encounter some resistance.

After making his demands known to the banker, Jim Tyson, Perk's lean, angular face underwent a change from bland ugliness to blank, white surprise and on to scarlet fury when Tyson refused.

"That's preposterous. Like hell I'll pay you scum a thousand dollars a day. Now get out of my office. I have important matters to deal with."

When the anger boiled up in him, Perk reached

across Tyson's desk, bunched the fat little banker's lapels in his huge, hard hands and jerked the man out of his swivel chair. Perk shook Tyson like a terrier would a rat.

"Lookie, you fat little bastard, I'm not askin', I'm tellin' ya. You cough up that thousand right now and be ready to spit it out again tomorrow afternoon and every day after that or you can make ready to join that two-bit law dog of yours over at the undertaker's place. Do I make myself clear?"

"Y-y-y-yes, sir. Yes, entirely clear," Tyson gasped. He rolled fear-glazed eyes to his chief teller who stood by the desk. "Ralph, will you see to this gentleman's needs?"

Ralph left and Tyson quailed in terror from Perk's onslaught, his eyes bugging and lips trembling. Satisfied, Perk let go of the banker, who slumped in an undignified heap on the floor behind his desk.

Evening came to Colby. Most citizens, those aware of the murder of their peace officers and the gang's declared control of town, huddled in tight-lipped fear behind their windows, dreading the worst. The townspeople knew the gang had made a second round of businesses, confiscating all the firearms and ammunition and taking them to the marshal's office to be placed under lock and key. They felt a numbing helplessness. Several men, though, had gathered in the back of Mayor Gilbert's feed and grain store.

In addition to the town counsel, Howie Wilkins, feeling nervous and out of place, was among them.

Mayor Gilbert had been in quiet, agitated conference with Howie, who constantly shook his head in a negative manner. The mayor broke off his argument and paced the floor. He stopped after a second and turned back to Howie.

"Now, damn it, Howie, we all know you have to run your store. But after all, if somebody don't take over as marshal and arrest Riney Stark and his gang, or chase them out of town, you might not have a business to operate anymore. None of us will."

Howie shook his head once more, his words falling quietly on the assembled, grim-faced men. "I hardly see why those men would want to take over my store." He tried a half-hearted chuckle to show he had no offense for anyone. "If they knew all the headaches it causes they'd be glad to leave it alone."

"This is no time for jokes, Howie," Jim Tyson snapped. "That wild-looking one came into the bank this afternoon wearin' a deputy's badge. He said they'd had an election. Stark was the new marshal and that the bank's protection insurance donation would be a thousand dollars a day. A thousand dollars! Said that would insure the bank never got robbed. What the hell do you call that but robbery? He collected for today right then. Nearly frightened my clerks to death."

Howie's pallid hand flew to his cheek. "Oh, my goodness. You mean to say you *paid him*? Why, my father taught me that by going along with outlaws only encouraged them to bolder deeds. My, my! This is serious."

"We all paid," Abe Goldman contributed glumly. "Every business in town. Except, from what I hear, your wife, Amy. They went to see her while you were over at Doc Parrish's arranging the funerals."

"Oh, my dear me. A-amy stood up to them, did she?"

"That she did," Mayor Gilbert said. "And showed a lot more spunk than the rest of us, I'm sorry to say. Chased that fancified one out with a broom."

"She did? Oh, dear. This could result in all sorts of trouble," Howie moaned in a complete reversal of his previous statement about resisting despotism. "Now why would she do a dangerous thing like that?"

"Inspired by your example, no doubt," the mayor boomed affably, every bit the cunning politician. "Now you see why we insist you are the man for the job. And, by your own admission just a moment ago, you are the only man in town with enough knowledge of outlaws to be capable of capturing them or running the lot out of town."

Howie blanched and canted his head to one side, as though expecting some powerful blow. He heaved a deep sigh, the mayor's words churning around in his head. At last he wet dry lips and answered:

"Well, gentlemen, might I suggest this as an alternative? Often a gang of this nature only needs to see that the entire populace is against them. This shows the miscreants that it is only a matter of time before the inevitable overtakes them.

"Mayor Gilbert, why not send a deputation of citizens down to the Idle Time, armed naturally, to try to talk sense with this Mr. Stark? Since you've now left open the opportunity for them to leave town without danger of arrest, it might work. Clint said Stark was an educated man. He must be a reasonable one, too, then. Say you go with eight or ten others. Then . . . if . . . if that fails . . . well, I'll . . . I'll consider taking over as marshal."

Mayor Gilbert puffed up with self-congratulations for reading his man so correctly. He reached out, took Howie's hand in his own two, and began to pump it enthusiastically.

"I'm proud of you, Howie. You made the right decision, you know."

"O-only for the duration of this affair, mind you, mayor. You know I abhore violence."

A small frown creased the mayor's fat, moon face for a moment, then he rallied a professional smile and began planning aloud. "Fine, Howie, fine. We realize your own feelings in the matter. We're proud of you, and we'll back you to the hilt."

Howie's words sounded plaintive, wistful. "You all backed Clint Rider to the hilt. His funeral is in the morning."

The pudgy mayor and equally chubby banker exchanged alarmed glances at this sudden show of faintheartedness on the part of their chosen champion. "Now, now, let's not dwell on past unpleasantnesses, Howie. I'm sure you can do what's needed. After all, you have always been the right man for this job. Why, everyone knows the son of Mason Wilkins would be the best choice for a lawman.

"Now, as to this citizens' committee, Howie. I think such a tactic needs much sober deliberation. A show of force usually inflames men of this stripe all the more. We need you, not a mob."

Amy Wilkins sat in a "thread-spool" design rocker in the small living room of the Wilkins house, doing embroidery appliqué on the wide hem folds of a set of pillow slips. Two ornate, milkglass kerosene lamps, one with a pale pink and rich green rose design on its base, illuminated the room. Amy used the pattern for the work of her flashing fingers and embroidery needle. She hummed to herself, an off-key, vexatious tune that betrayed her impatience. The distant sound of sporadic gunshots from the Idle Time Saloon only added to her irritation. She looked up anxiously when Howie entered the front door.

"Well, what did Mayor Gilbert want, Howard?"

Howie Wilkins hung his derby on one of the curved hat hooks of the silent butler in the hallway and examined his image in the long, bevel-edged mirror. He wondered idly if he should buff the dust from his shoes before entering the carpeted living room. He pondered more whether his decision showed on his face. Howie turned slowly and looked thoughtfully at his wife.

"He offered me Clint's job."

Amy stopped her work, letting the pillow slip rest in her lap. Her eyes lit with the ambition burning within her. "And what did you tell him?"

"I simply said that I would think it over," Howie answered.

Sudden anger at this apparent frustration of her ambition caused Amy to make a sharp, intemperate reply. "Think it over! What is there to think over? The first opportunity you've had to assert yourself in this dreary community; the *only* chance we have to rise politically and you have to stop and think about it?"

"But, my dear . . ."

Amy didn't hear him. She went on, enraptured with her visions, born of frustration and ambition. "You could be councilman next, then mayor, the territorial legislature. Who knows? When New Mexico becomes a state, even the Congres . . . or Senator. Power, Howard, power. That's what moves the world, and the Wilkins family is accustomed to the exercise of power."

Howie drew himself up abruptly. His own conflicting emotions brought him to the edge of actual defiance of his wife's grandiose illusions. "Now you sound like Papa."

Amy stood, a surprised look on her face. Her forgotten piecework fell to the floor, and she stepped idly over it to walk rapidly across the living room to where her husband stood poised in the doorway. Before she could voice her hot retort, Howie went on:

"You know we both agree about the use of violence and that civilized people do not resort to such crude solutions. Well . . . I mean," he stammered, at once unsure of himself. "Now you act as though Papa's ways were right, after all."

"We aren't living in the East, Howard. This is the frontier and the people are barbarians. The use of violence to gain power is the only means they respect. Maybe if you had listened to your father more, things would be different around here."

Howie's fears asserted themselves over his earlier resolution. "*If* I had listened to my father . . . that would have been me killed out there instead of Clint Rider."

Fear of losing her control over Howie lashed fury through Amy's body, and she struggled to master her seething emotions. Her ambition for prominence and power could be destroyed by a wrong word, she realized. She decided at last to use guile and flattery instead of her potent, sharp-edged tongue.

"Howard, oh, Howard, I would never have married you if I didn't love you. You know that, darling, don't you? I saw in you more than another vapid Yale undergraduate.

"I saw a great deal more than others did. I think . . . what I found in you was a reflection of your father: his constancy, his courage, his strength. I knew you were a man destined to rise high in affairs of state, to achieve prominence and respect. And I thought of you as the bravest man I knew. Oh, don't destroy my dream now. Please don't take away all I ever hoped for, planned for."

Howie's rigid mask throttled the words in Amy's throat. He looked at his wife in utter astonishment. The events of the past days had already pushed his mind beyond its capacity to accommodate the hard realities of the frontier. Now his wife's revelation of her feelings and ambitions left him dizzied and confused—and not a little angry. He spoke in a hollow, strangled tone:

"And all you've schemed for, my dear? Do you think me such a starry-eyed dreamer to be totally unaware of the purpose behind all your manipulations? Can't you understand? I don't want position, influence, power. All I want is to be left alone to run my store and live in peace."

Stunned, Amy rocked backward as though from a physical blow. Tears filled her eyes and ran down her face. "Oh, Howard, Howard, forgive me," she wailed. She took tottering steps until she fell into his arms. Sobs shook her shoulders, breaking up her words into a disjointed jumble.

"I . . . never real . . . ized . . . h-how much . . . you . . . how strongly . . . you felt a-about . . . it. I . . . only wanted what was . . . best for . . . us . . . truly, I . . . d-d-id."

Howie wiped a hand across his brow, removed his gold-rimmed spectacles and industriously polished them over Amy's heaving shoulders. In the silence that followed Amy's outburst, he found it hard to speak. At last, his newly formed resolve to refuse the mayor's petition dissolved by Amy's wash of emotion, he gently disengaged her clinging arms and set her away from him. In soft, earnest words, he told her the real outcome of the meeting.

"I . . . didn't tell you everything, dear. The mayor made me promise to take the job on at least a temporary basis. Until the Riney Stark gang has been dealt with. I was uncertain about how you might feel in light of what happened to Clint, and by the time I reached home I had . . . had decided to decline. But now . . ." Howie cleared his throat and pushed past Amy, walking to the center of the living room.

"Well, now, to be honest with you, I think that if . . . ah, with a posse behind me, I imagine it could be done. But Mayor Gilbert said I should do it alone. You don't want me to . . . to get killed for nothing, do you?"

"Do what you must, Howard," Amy replied in a small voice. "The details of how you accomplish it can be worked out later. But don't you see, darling, You are the person who can stop these men. This is your chance to exert yourself in the community and . . . and, damn it, you can't afford not to take advantage of it."

Chapter 14

Rev. Adam Brenski adjusted the pages containing his notes for the sermon on the slanted lectern in the pulpit and gazed out over the congregation. Mourners for the marshal for the most part, he thought. Faces he'd never before seen inside the walls of Colby's Bethany Church of the Good Shepherd.

The Reverend Mr. Brenski's dark, curly-haired good looks, black, snapping eyes and square jaw in a round face, on a slightly over-large head, belied his calling to the cloth, but his slender, spare build, long aesthetic fingers and pallid, uncallused hands spoke of his profession unerringly. He smiled a sad, professional smile as the organ music completed its dirge.

"Beloved sisters and brothers in Christ, we are gathered together today in the sight of Almighty God to pay our last respects to Clinton Norris Rider, a fellow communicant in the mystical body and blood of our Lord, Jesus Christ," Adam Brenski began. The reverend's sermon continued for several minutes, concluding with what he believed would be a thundering condemnation of violence and a spiritual uplift for the congregation.

"Violence begets violence, and those who live by the sword, shall . . . ah . . . er . . ." he stumbled. The marshal had, after all, been enforcing the law and hired to do so at that. Perhaps his choice of words had been unfortunate. He made a rapid mental editing of his last paragraph and finished on a less treacherous thought. "The Lord giveth and the Lord taketh away. Blessed be the name of the Lord."

"Amen," the congregation chorused.

The organ began again, a well known hymn. While voices joined in, off-key but sincere, the large double doors opened at the back, and a squat, dark-skinned, bowlegged man entered. He strode through the vestibule and started down the center aisle toward Clint Rider's coffin. As he passed each line of pews, the voices of the singers faltered and dropped out.

"What is the meaning of this?" Brenski demanded in his best sepulchral tone, eyes glaring at the gun-totting, ill-clothed image of a savage standing before him.

"I've come to bury my friend," Davey Two-Knife replied in a low, even voice.

"Our lately departed, and most beloved, marshal was no friend of you or your kind."

"The hell he wasn't. By now that rum-dum Coulter must have spread it all over town that we was kids together, Clint an' me. So I'll pay my last respects, and you can get on with the funeral."

Adam Brenski felt anger to the soles of his feet. He wanted to lash out with those big hands of his and smash the arrogant face of this killer who stood so brazenly in his church. He had used them to great effect in the time before his calling and even during the years in the seminary. But now was neither the time nor the place, he reminded himself. He shook a fist, in the best fire and brimstone manner, at Davey Two-Knife and called on all his talents as an orator.

"This is the house of God. Your presence in this place offends Him and these good people. Kindly get out of here."

Davey looked around him, his brow wrinkling. "I don't see this God of yours around here to do anythin' about it, and none o' these so-called *good* people have balls enough to toss me out, so I think I'll stay."

"The funeral is over. We were about to start the procession to the cemetary."

"Don't let me stop you, reverend. I'll just go along then."

Adam Brenski stepped out of the pulpit, walked past the communion rail and down the aisle to where Davey stood. "You are an abomination. You and your kind shall burn in hellfire. Remove yourself from the presence of the righteous and hide from the wrath of God!" he thundered. Then he continued in a whisper heard only by Davey, "Or I'll kick your ass."

The briefest of smiles turned up the corner's of Davey's mouth, and a twinkle lighted his eyes while he evaluated this cocky, bantam rooster of a preacher and gave him respect.

Angry mutters rose on both sides of the aisle. Davey broke the reverend's fixed stare, and looked around at the stern, hate-filled faces and felt a twinge of discomfort. He couldn't get them all, were they to decide to rush him. He had no desire to be the central figure in a lynching. Yet something inside cried out his remorse and grief. He had to brave them long enough to say a final farewell to Clint. He bit his lower lip and refrained from any further reply. The preacher's unexpected show of strength and a different nature encouraged him. He stepped around the cleric, and marched silently up the remainder of the aisle and bent low over the coffin. To his surprise, no one moved to interfere.

Clint looked to be merely asleep, perhaps a bit paler than in life, but not the usual waxy green-tinged paleness of a corpse. The undertaker had done as ordered, Davey thought, pleased. His lips barely moved when he spoke.

"Good-bye, Clint, old pard. I . . . I'll miss you." Emotion choked Davey's words and his eyes filled with tears. He said nothing else and strode rapidly out of the church.

Three of the gang loafed round the Idle Time Saloon. Riney, Charlie, and Pearly sat at a table while the latter two played a game of two-hand monte. Their collection chores completed for the day, little else presented itself for distraction. They looked up when the bat wings flew open noisily and Davey entered.

"How was the funeral, Davey?" Charlie asked smirking.

"They threw me out! The bastards nearly didn't let me go along to the cemetary till the undertaker told 'em it was me paid for it all." For the first time, Davey noticed the badge pinned on Charlie's vest. He frowned.

Charlie's nervous glance took in what Davey scowled at, and he hastened to explain. "You mean this? Well, we talked it over. Seein' as how the marshal became deceased so suddenlike along with all his deputies, we felt the town needed law and order. So, while you were seein' to the buryin', we held an election. Made Riney the new marshal, every one else is a dep'ty. Come over here and I'll pin on your badge."

Davey hesitated a moment, the memory of Clint's dead face still fresh in his mind. Then he shrugged, cast his lot with the others and walked to where Charlie sat.

"Sure. Why the hell not?"

"By God, I don't believe it," Perk Perkins exploded as he crashed through the swinging doors. The gang turned as one to face him.

"What's goin' on, Perk?" Riney inquired, tipping back the low-drawn brim of his Stetson.

"Them people over at the bank. They must be plumb crazy. I went over for the usual collection, like always. That damn teller closed this little bitty grill in my face and tells me they ain't payin' anymore. Says there's a new marshal in town, and he advised them . . . advised them, do you believe that? . . . not to pay. Told me to get out of there, pronto."

"What did you do?" Charlie inquired, his pig eyes bright with excitement.

"What do you expect? I slapped open that fancy grill and grabbed Mr. Teller by his scrawny turkey neck and shook him till his false teeth fell out on the counter. He squawked and yelled and flopped around a lot until I let him go. Then he crab-walked back to Tyson's office and had a palaver."

"Go on," Riney urged.

"Well, I didn't want to be left out of nothin' important, so I shoved through the little swingin' gate and gets myself over to Tyson's door. Good thing I did, too, 'cause when I kicked it in, that runt of a clerk and ol' fat-ass Tyson were gettin' shootin' irons outta a cabinet."

"Did you shoot 'em, Perk?" Charlie asked.

"Naw. Just scared hell outta them and made the collection the way I should have in the first place. Brought along the guns, too."

"Good, Perk. Now, what about this new marshal that's supposed to be in town?"

"Don't know much. Only that he's the son of some former hard-nosed law dog named Mason Wilkins. Supposed to be meaner than a wildcat with barbed wire around his tail. He's gonna run our butts outta town or slap us behind bars."

The gang laughed uproariously at this suggestion.

"I'm plumb scared shitless," Charlie wheezed through his merriment.

Howie Wilkins felt uncomfortable with the heavy weight of his father's old Colt strapped around his waist. He had fumbled about his person, unsure of what to do with the badge until he decided to pin it on his apron. He stood in the center of his general store feeling miserable and not a little afraid.

"Howard, get rid of that ridiculous thing," Amy demanded when she came out of the storage room.

"Th-the gun, my dear?" Howie inquired, uncertain.

"No, that silly apron. When you go to do your duty as marshal, you don't want to look like a shopkeeper."

"But that's what I am," Howie protested. "Merely because I have agreed to do as Mayor Gilbert wishes, doesn't mean I've become a moustachioed, buckskin-wearing Bill Hickock. I don't see why I should dress the part."

"How-ard," Amy weedled. "When you step out that door, you represent the town of Colby, not just Wilkins's mercantile. It is important that you impress upon those men the importance of your mission."

"It's impressed enough on me," Howie lamented in a quiet voice.

"What did you say?" Amy demanded crossly.

"Well, I . . . suppose I had better go and do it."

"Yes, Howard, that you should."

Howie Wilkins walked to the double glass-paneled doors of his store and emerged onto the plank walk. He grimaced at the sight of the boards covering the broken window and, for the moment, it gave him new resolve. He adjusted the sagging loop of the gun belt and stepped into the street.

With a laggard gait, he started across toward the Idle Time. His pulse seemed to pound visibly in his temples. He hesitated before stepping up on the boardwalk that formed the porch of the establishment. Once more he hefted the thick leather gun belt, swallowed with effort and proceeded toward the bat wings.

He reached out to one swinging door and grasped it firmly. Blood still stained the wood and the planks of the walk. Howie glanced around and noted that a crowd had already begun to form. He sighed heavily, with resignation, and pushed his way inside.

The whole gang sat at one central table playing a hand of five-card stud. Perk peered myopically at his hole card and tossed a double eagle into the pot.

"An' that'll make a twenty dollar raise."

"Too steep for me," Charlie protested, folding his hand.

"I'll stay," Riney muttered around the stub of a cigar.

The gang leader seemed unaware of Howie's approach. The small storekeeper walked on the balls of his feet, wincing when a floorboard creaked alarmingly. He stopped a few feet behind Riney's broad back and waited for the final card to be dealt, bets made and the winner, Perk, to expose his hand. Howie's voice, when he at last forced himself to speak, came out high pitched and weak.

"Uh . . . Mr. Stark? Uh . . . I'm here to tell you men that . . . uh . . ."

Riney reacted to the squeaky voice, turning in his chair to glare balefully at its owner. "Yeah, what is it, sonny?" Riney seemed surprised to find a man, and not a boy, facing him.

Howie cleared his throat and tried to look stern. "Uh . . . the good citizens of . . . uh . . . Colby have asked me to . . . er . . . inform you that you have . . . uh . . . two hours to . . . ah, that is, leave our town on your own . . . uh . . . power. After that you . . . you will be dealt with accordingly. And that is . . . uh . . . final. Do I . . . make myself clear?"

Riney looked the short, timid-looking storekeeper up and down, incredulity on his face. Unbelievable! He couldn't accept that this was happening. Slowly his lips began to twitch, then curl into a smile. Riney opened his mouth wide and let out great, deep pearls of laughter. The others joined in, Charlie breaking off to crow like a rooster and flap his folded arms in imitation of wings.

In the midst of their hilarity, even Howie put on a shy, puzzled smile. Riney and Perk climbed from their chairs, still chortling, and stood beside Howie, towering over him. They looked down at him and began to guffaw again.

"You mean . . ." Perk began between peals of laughter which continued to interrupt while he spoke, "to tell us that you . . . that you . . . are the great . . . law dog? The best that they had left . . . to send . . . send over here?"

"This is rich. Oh, this is real rich!" Riney managed to choke out between bellows of mirth. He bent down toward Howie, peering closely as though at a specimen caught in the wild.

"Does your mommy know you play in the street with real guns?"

Charlie chortled, waggling his fingers at the side of his head.

Riney grabbed Howie by one ear and bent until his nose nearly touched the frightened storekeeper's cheek. "Hummm. Well, little boy, you seem to have dirty ears. Do you think your mommy would like you going out with dirty ears?" He turned to the others. "I think he needs a bath. What about it, boys? Don't he need a bath?"

The gang suddenly stood and clustered around the hapless Howie. The diminutive merchant began to tremble, partly from fear, but also from rage at the insulting manner in which he was being treated. They had no right to do this!

Humiliating; apparently not even concerned about their eviction from the town. He tried to smile fleetingly and reassert his authority, only to find himself whisked off his feet, carried by the back of his collarless shirt and seat of his pants. He flailed helplessly and fought the inevitable that their banter implied.

Out in the street, the gang crossed to the water trough, Pearly and Davey now holding the squirming Howie between them.

Amid their loud, raucous shouts, they made great ceremony of hoisting Howie high in the air and trouncing him deep under the green-slimed water of the horse tank. There they held him for several long moments, drawing him up briefly to sputter and gasp for air. Then they repeated their action, drubbing Howie like a piece of laundry.

The crowd that had gathered earlier emitted shocked exclamations but stepped hastily back out of the gang's way. Riney noticed that some of these "good people" of Colby had joined in the laughter at the little storekeeper's expense. The dowsing continued for several minutes until the gang tired of their sport.

Perk hauled the dripping Howie out of the trough and stood him in the dust of the street. Howie had lost his derby and gold-rim glasses. His clothes hung in sodden wrinkles about his body, and his high button shoes squelched with the sound of water that sloshed over the tops. Perk made a show at brushing Howie down.

"There now, all clean." A sudden idea came to Perk when he noticed Charlie scurry up behind Howie and bend low on hands and knees. He snapped out violently with both open palms, struck Howie soundly in his pigeon-breasted chest and drove him over Charlie's back. The two outlaws rolled the helpless merchant around until he wore a thick coat of mud.

"Hey there," Perk bellowed in Howie's face. "How you get so dirty again? We only just cleaned you up."

"Yeah, mud ball," Charlie chided. "Best you scurry on home so's Mommy can wash you off again or she'll get mad and spank."

Howie groped dimly to find his way, face smudged and smarting with humiliation. He stumbled when the forgotten gun belt slipped to his knees. Behind his retreating form the gang bellowed their derisive laughter. Before he'd made it halfway across the street, Riney crossed to Howie and jerked him around by one shoulder.

"Now you hear me good, boy. I don't take to nobody tellin' me to leave any town. Onliest reason we didn't gun you down was 'cause you looked so little and pitiful. You best get out of here now and leave law enforcin' to the big boys, you hear? An' don't you or none of them panty-waist townies come sniffin' around here again."

"I . . . I . . ." Howie's shoulders slumped and his head drooped until his chin touched his chest, and he shuffled off toward the general mercantile. Amy chose that moment to step out on the boardwalk, attracted by the loud noises in the street. She took in the bedraggled figure of her husband limping toward her, and her eyes flashed with fury. Her dignity outraged, in that moment she felt both pity and contempt for Howie. She stamped one small foot on the wide plank and shook a fist at the gang.

"You fiends," she yelled. "You'll pay for this. This is shameful! Don't you have any shred of decency?"

Riney tipped his hat in a gallant gesture. "We're decent enough to those who treats us in kind, ma'am."

Amy emitted a long, frustrated, "Oooh!" and whirled to follow her defeated and demeaned husband inside the store. Behind her, the gang took in her slender, little form and exchanged grinning, lustful looks.

"Say, boys, that's about the prettiest li'l thing I've seen in a long time," Charlie drawled.

"You're dead right, Charlie," Pearly added. He dabbed a finger at the thin line of his moustache. "I'd like to see more of her myself . . . a lot more."

With mutual, unspoken agreement, all but Riney nodded among themselves. Leaving their boss behind, they started across the street toward the store.

Amy Wilkins stood behind the counter, pen in hand, and worked on the ledger Howie had been attending to before his encounter with the gang. She looked up, startled, at the tinkle of the small bell over the door. Her eyes narrowed slightly when she recognized the outlaws standing inside the open portal.

"What do you want now?" she demanded. "Haven't you done enough?"

The gang grinned at her, giggling and nudging one another like bashful boys at a church social. They cast hungry looks at Amy that needed no words. Suddenly frightened, Amy took a step backward, and a fluttering hand flew to the bodice of her dress.

"I . . . I asked you what you wanted."

Perk closed the door firmly, locked it and pulled down the green shades. He peeled back his thin lips in a yellow-toothed leer. "Why ain't that fairly obvious right now, little lady?"

"Yeah. Where's that little pullet of a husband of yourn?" Charlie licked his pudgy lips and cast glances around the store.

"I . . . I . . . He went home to change his clothes . . ." Her voice trailed off when she realized the terrible mistake she'd made in revealing she was alone in the store. She gulped back a sob of fear and decided to bluster her way out.

"He's coming back with his shotgun. If I were you, I'd be a long way from here when he does." She took a hesitant sidestep. "You get out of here, hear me? Get off these premises."

Charlie groped one hand at his crotch. "We sure will, ma'am. Right after we git what we come for."

Amy's nerve faltered again. She began to move away from the counter that separated her from the gang, her body trembling with fear. Her lips quivered when she raged at them again.

"Get out of here, you animals!"

Chapter 15

Amy Wilkins made a serious tactical error then.

Her eyes wide with fearful knowledge of the gang's intent, she darted toward the back room of the store, then changed her course abruptly and ran along behind the long side counter, at the end of which an opening provided quick access to the front door. She failed to make it even halfway.

Charlie Bell leaped up on the counter, scattering and breaking the glass jars of candy, upsetting a keg of nails and bursting several prepackaged pound bags of flour and sugar. He bounded onto the floor behind Amy and grabbed her by the shoulders, drew her close to him and turned her around.

"Waaahoo! I got her! That makes me first, don't it, Perk? Huh, Pearly? Davey? Me first, huh?"

Amy began to struggle but Charlie proved too strong for her. In her terror she abandoned all attempts to project a calm demeanor. Tears ran down her cheeks, and she helplessly pounded her small fists on Charlie's fat-padded chest.

"Please let me go. Oh, please! I'm . . . I'm a married woman. I . . . I . . . please don't."

Charlie lifted her from her feet and began to stumble toward the open doorway to the storage room at the rear. He rubbed the coarse stubble of his two-day growth of beard raspingly against her cheek, which brought forth a yelp of pain, and he giggled into her ear.

"You bein' married an' all oughtta make this easy for you. You know all about it, don't you, pretty lady?"

In desperation, Amy violently brought up her knee into Charlie's crotch, mashing into his exposed testicles. Charlie cried out and his hold loosened. In a flash Amy took advantage of the situation to break free. Her mind numbed by unthinking panic, she rushed behind the other counter only to stumble to a halt, her throat working convulsively to produce a scream that would not come, when she saw her avenue of escape blocked by Pearly and Davey.

Amy glanced wildly from the menacing figures before her to Charlie, who, doubled over by his pain, still advanced toward her. Perk suddenly closed in on her, reached across the counter and grabbed Amy. He pulled her to him, his face molded into a triumphant leer. One eye looked one way, the other another.

"I got her! Charlie lost her and I got her back. Now I'm first."

Despair and defeat settled on Amy, though she continued to struggle and sob while Perk scooped her up in his arms and carried her through the doorway. Behind him, the other gang members began to flip coins to determine their turns.

Late afternoon sun cast long shadows into the streets of Colby when Howie Wilkins, now cleaned up and dressed in fresh clothing, walked toward the general mercantile. He bravely tried to whistle a tune in an attempt to appear casual and indifferent in the face of his neighbors' scorn. He swung into Main Street with a brisk stride and headed directly to the front of his store.

A frown creased his forehead when he noticed the doors closed and the narrow green blinds drawn. Amy hadn't come home. Why had she shut up the shop? He tried the door and found it unlocked. He stepped inside, his feeling of puzzlement and unease increasing, and he called to his wife.

"Amy? Oh, Amy, love?"

Only silence greeted him. Howie apprehensively stepped further into the room.

"Amy," he called again. His eyes swept the display area and stopped at the signs of destruction. A cold fear crawled over his body at sight of the broken jars, scattered nails, and white dust lying over all. He hurried to the counter, eyes wide, lips atremble.

The ledger Amy had been working on lay on the floor, pages torn and wrinkled from being trod upon, a film of flour covering it like lace filigree. He bent and retrieved it, uncertain of its meaning, yet fearful he already knew. Something had happened to Amy, something violent and—and—

Howie halted his runaway thoughts and looked up in numb shock at the sound of soft sobbing that came from the back room.

Hesitantly at first, his feet dragging, Howie headed

toward the sound. He passed through the doorway into the storage area and halted, mouth open and working, gagging on the sour bile that rose in his throat.

Amy lay sprawled among the barrels and boxes of their reserve stock. Her dress had been torn from her, and her petticoats rumpled high up her legs, bunched under her bruised, bare hips. Her underdrawers had been ripped off and cast aside and, against his will, Howie found his eyes drawn to her scratched and battered naked thighs. His voice croaked as he cried out.

"A-Amy? Oh, my God, Amy . . ."

"Uh, th-they . . . had their way with me, Howard! *Raped* me. Do you . . . do you have any idea what that means to a woman?" Her voice rose to a hysterical pitch while her trembling hands explored her abused and battered body. "I'm ruined. Ruined! The people of Colby will say I should have fought harder, that I made it too easy. They'll say I should have made them kill me rather than submit. Oh, God, what do they know?"

Her face had gone lumpy with punches. A large black and yellow bruise formed under one eye, and her body bore signs of a savage beating. She shuddered at her own touch, as though her body had become a repulsive thing. "Submit! Does it look like I submitted, Howard?"

Howie rushed forward and sought to cover his wife's nakedness with her torn garments, his eyes filled with horror. Amy recoiled from him and thrust pleading hands between them.

"No! Stay away! I don't want any man to touch me. Do you hear me? I never want to be touched again. I . . . I . . ." Amy broke off to utter a piercing, soul-wrenching scream. "Oh, God. Oh, Howard, why? Why?"

Howie cringed back, afraid of appearing to reject Amy in the manner she feared the townsfolk would do, and he was equally disturbed by her refusal of his ministrations. Despite her current state, Amy's words lay on him like a scalding condemnation. At last, shoulders slumped in resignation, he turned his back on her and walked unsteadily from the room.

A grim and somber group met in the back room of the feed and grain store. The gathering, called by Mayor Gilbert, seemed at a stalemate. They had offered their condolences to Howie over his humiliation by the gang and the rape of his wife. Old Doc Allen had spread word of it all over town after he had gone to the Wilkins's home to treat her. Now, by unspoken accord, all heads turned to Howie.

"We realize the mistake we made in expecting you to handle this alone, Howie," Mayor Gilbert said hesitantly. "I mean, after all, these men are hardened desperados. Your wisdom in suggesting a citizen's committee was right after all. I . . . all of us are ready to stand behind you now. We'll march on the saloon and drive those thieving, murderous devils out into the open. There'll be a hangin' for sure."

"Rapists," Howie said softly into the long silence that followed Bryce Gilbert's speech. "You forgot to call them rapists." Howie turned on the gathered men, his usually placid face black with anger. "None of this would have happened . . . to Amy, to me . . . to this town . . . if you would have had courage enough to make a show of force when Clint first went to arrest them."

Mayor Gilbert gave careful attention to the toes of his black, highly polished shoes. The other council members, with the exception of Miles Parrish, who gave them a sardonic, I-told-you-so smile, intently studied the walls and ceiling, equally unable to meet Howie's furious gaze. Jim Tyson, at last, spoke for all of them.

"We know that, Howie, and we're sorry."

Howie paced to the center of the room and glowered down at the banker, the rage on his face replaced by a look of disgust. "Yes, Jim. You're a sorry lot, all right. The only one of you to offer help, to act like a man, was Miles. Yet now, when you're hurt in the one way that counts, in the pocketbook, you are suddenly ready to form a vigilante committee and string up Stark and his gang to the nearest tree. After what has happened, why do you expect me to go at the head of this vengeful delegation? Didn't you get enough laughs this afternoon?"

"Now, Howie, that's hardly fair," Mayor Gilbert began, blustering as usual.

"Fair! What the hell has fair got to do with it? Has anything been *fair* since the Riney Stark gang rode into town?"

The councilmen and the mayor cringed back from the sudden, unexpected vehemence in Howie's words. Gilbert opened his mouth to interrupt, but lapsed into deflated, sagjawed silence when Howie thundered at them:

"I'll tell you how we're going to handle this problem, and it will be done that way or not at all. You, Mr.

Mayor, are going to be at the head of this little committee. That's right, out front ahead of us all. Then, you fine, courageous members of the town council, will be in line behind him. Everyone armed to the teeth, mind you. Then I'll bring up the rear, where I can keep an eye on everything that is happening. It would be a good idea to have every able-bodied man in town, over the age of fifteen, back of me, ready to shoot on command. It's the only way that offers any hope of success."

"Now, Howie, I'm not so certain—"

"What's the matter, Mr. Mayor?" Howie interrupted sarcastically. "You didn't seem to lack any courage in sending another man out to be trounced in a water trough and rolled in the dirt. You appear to have survived the ordeal of my wife's rape without turning a hair. Why not take this opportunity to shine in the eyes of your constituents? After all, there *is* an election coming up next year. Wouldn't hurt to make yourself more visible to the voters."

"Howard," the chubby politician wailed.

"I'm not finished yet. We'll want plenty of rope around. We'll hold a trial right there in the middle of the street and hang those bastards from the balcony of the Idle Time."

"My God, Howie, the territorial governor would never countenance something like that!"

A bitter laugh broke from Howie's lips. "What's he going to do, resurrect them after we've done the job? If you want a citizen's safety committee to deal with Stark, Mr. Mayor, this is the only way. You'd better accept that, because you're going to be presiding if we have to hog-tie you and drag you there." Howie turned to the others. "Go get guns, lots of them, and men and some rope."

Amy Wilkins sat in an unlighted room, rocking listlessly in her padded chair. She had cried herself dry long ago, and her sobs had abated into small, mewing sounds. The aches of her body had diminished to small twinges, all except for a burning numbness between her thighs.

"Oh, Christ!" Amy cried aloud when the thought asserted itself in her agony-dulled mind. "What if I'm pregnant by . . . by one of those animals?"

New tremors shook her body, and a cold, determined realization took possession of her being.

Piano music tinkled gaily from the interior of the Idle Time Saloon. The professional laughter of the soiled doves was made even shriller by their fear of the tough, dangerous men whose company they were forced to keep. Charlie Bell sat sprawled in a chair, one floozy sitting astride his lap, his hands clutching the rounded mounds of her buttocks. He was half drunk, a dribble of spittle trickling from the corner of his grinning mouth. No one else paid him mind.

Riney sat alone at a table in the dark corner of the room, under the stair. He seemed to brood. He'd said little since the rest of the gang had joined in raping the storekeeper's wife. His tastes didn't include such activities, and he had felt at the time, even more so now, that allowing them to indulge their lust had been a mistake.

His original idea had been to slowly bleed this town

dry while resting up and to let enough time pass to cool off Arizona Territory so they could return. Now, their precipitous action might have spoiled all that. He looked up when Perk reeled over from the bar, one arm around the slender waist of a gaudily dressed girl.

"Shay . . . R-Riney, ol' buddy. Y'all want to dip yer wick in this tasty morsel?"

Riney shrugged, indicating his indifference toward the demands of the flesh. Perk started to say more, but Davey interrupted when he called from the doorway. "Looks like we're gonna have some more company, Riney."

Perk jerked his head around. "Tha' little twerp from this afternoon?"

"Don't see him," Davey replied. "There's a whole batch just turned onto Main Street, headed this way. They're armed, and it looks like they mean us no good."

Riney rose and took command. "Charlie, get that frump off your lap. Go upstairs and slip out on the balcony. Keep low and don't let those townies see you. Take your Winchester along, too, dummy. Now, Perk, Pearly, Davey, go out the back and head to each end of the alley. When you hear me talkin' to whoever is out there, swing in behind them and at the far end of the street. So's we got the drop on the bunch."

"Right, boss," the outlaws chorused. Each man moved to his assignment.

Behind the bar, Cactus Jack McGowen watched with narrowed eyes. He idly wiped at a glass, long ago polished, and worked his jaws in frustration. Riney moved with smooth, quiet grace to a spot beside the bat wings, drew his sixgun and held it ready. In a moment, the saloon had emptied of all the others. McGowen silently put aside his towel and the glass and sidled toward the end of the bar, his gaze never leaving the dominant figure of Riney Stark. When the voice of Mayor Gilbert called from outside, McGowen took a deep breath and began counting to himself.

"Riney Stark! You and your men are under arrest. Come out with your hands up. We have enough guns here to blast you to doll rags."

"Don't figger that's much of an advantage, feller," Riney drawled. He spun into the center of the doorway and pushed aside the bat wings. Preceded by his Navy Colts, Riney strode with heavy, solid steps onto the porch. He paused, as though startled by the massive showing of strength behind the mayor.

"Fixin' to have a party, Mr. Mayor?" Riney bantered.

"Yeah, a necktie party for you and that rabble of yourn," a belligerent young man yelled from among the tight-packed ranks behind Howie.

"I'm stung by your unkind words, sir," Riney said while he stepped out into the street, facing Mayor Gilbert with less than six feet between them. He looked beyond the muttering, angry mob to see Davey and Pearly walk out into the intersection and advance half a block toward the unsuspecting townsmen.

"Throw down your guns, Stark. I'm warning you."

"If it comes to threats, Mr. Mayor, I have one of my own. You'd best all lay down them irons and skedaddle off to home where it's safe. The night air's bad for a feller, they say."

"Like hell we will," one man cried from the rear of the crowd. He threw a Winchester to his shoulder, the muzzle leveling at Riney's chest.

Smoke and flame belched from one muzzle of the Greener twelve gauge in Pearly's hands. Pellets bit into flesh, and the man with the Winchester dropped it before he fell to the ground, stone dead. The gent beside him, a clerk in the bank, collapsed, too, and writhed in the dirt from the agony of his wounds.

"Shuck them irons, boys," Riney ordered again. Behind him, Perk came into view, holding another shotgun. A glance told Riney that Perk had a commanding field of fire. "That was just one barrel. You want to try for two?"

Charlie Bell giggled insanely and rose from behind the obscuring saloon sign. "An' I can drill the eyeballs outta you peckerwoods before a one of you can unleather a sixgun."

"Aces full, mayor. Looks like you loose this hand. Now, gentlemen, if you'll be so kind, get shed of them guns and do it fast before my friends here ventilate all your hides."

Reluctantly, one at a time, then in pairs and threes, firearms began to thud into the dust of the street. When the last man rid himself of his weapon, Riney gestured toward the residential part of town with the muzzle of his Colt.

"Y'all get on for home, now, ya hear? Count among your blessings that you still got whole hides and . . . in the future, keep the hell out of our way."

Mayor Gilbert hung his head and walked away, his shoulders slumped in defeat. Unable to meet the eyes of his fellow citizens, he trudged through their ranks and left the scene of his humiliation. His pace increased the further he got from the threat of the outlaws' guns. Slowly, silently, the townspeople followed him, leaving the corpse and the wounded man behind with their weapons.

With a whoop of joy the gang descended on the piles of discarded firearms and gathered them up. They carried their booty inside the saloon and dumped the guns on tables. Riney paused at the bat wings long enough to shout at the retreating backs:

"Better send the undertaker . . . and the doc to take care of these two. We don't want 'em stinkin' up our clean air."

Charlie was first to notice that Jack McGowen had used the distraction of the mayor's committee to make good an escape. No matter, he thought, walking behind the bar. He set bottles out for each man.

"Looks like I got me a new job, boys. Belly up and have one on the house." The gang quickly complied. Perk turned to the frightened, nearly exhausted piano player.

"Give us a tune, boy. What say . . . 'Lorena'?"

"Aw, who wants a sorrowful thing like that?" Charlie protested. "It al'ays makes me cry."

"Play it," Davey demanded. "That's the kind of mood I'm in, too."

The frightened man hastened to comply, one eye nervously on Perk and Davey, the other on the sulking Charlie. From his place at the short end of the bar, Riney hoisted his glass and called the others to order.

"We-ell, boys, fun's fun, but it all has to end sometime. It looks like those townies have found their balls again."

"Lost 'em, seems more like to me." Perk guffawed.

"Could be, Perk," Riney allowed. "But they could

grow new ones mighty fast. No cause to tempt fate. I say we empty out that bank tomorrow. Same for all the other places. Then we hit the trail for more hospitable surroundings. What do you think boys?"

"Fine and dandy by me, boss," Perky drawled. "What say we head for Texas?"

"Suits," Perk agreed briefly.

"A change of scene might help, Riney," Davey admitted, his eyes cast at the sawdust mounds on the floor.

"Aw, hell, Riney," Charlie began, then gulped and changed his tune. "Whatever you say, boss. Whatever you say."

"Good, then. We're all agreed. Have yourselves a fling tonight, then, boys. Early in the morning we're gonna clean this place out."

"I don't know about the rest of you," Pearly purred warmly while he walked to where a pert-faced, pug-nosed saloon girl sat on the edge of the bar. "But I could use my ashes hauled."

He looped a arm around the slender waist of the soiled dove and lifted her, squealing with delight, from the mahogany counter. She couldn't have been over sixteen years old, Riney thought, as he watched Pearly nuzzle her in the hollow of her throat. The dapper outlaw whispered in her ear, and they strolled toward the door, arms around each other.

Behind the amorous pair a chorus of whistles and catcalls rose. Charlie, as usual, whooped louder than anyone.

"Whooee! That Pearly! He's some ladies' man. Don't think he's ever got too much."

"There ain't no such thing as *too much*, Charlie," Perk yelled back.

"Aw, go on now," Charlie spluttered, embarrassed at his own limited ability to perform and his knowledge that the gang knew of it.

Pearly and his girl walked down the center of the street, hands gently touching, stroking each other's eager body. He leaned to her, kissed her on one ear and poked his tongue into the pink, delicate opening.

"Don't!" she cried out peevishly. "That's nasty. Besides, you get me too all-fired worked up, and we'll have to do it right here in the middle of town."

"At high noon, honey," Pearly assured her. "In front of God and everybody."

She gave him a light, playful slap on the cheek. "That's awful. What would the good people in town say about that?" She started to giggle, then stopped to point to a recessed space between two buildings. "There's my place," the young prostitute told him. "Up those stairs. We can be alone all night."

"All night," Pearly repeated. "That's the way I like it, honey pot. Lead the way."

They turned into the blackness of the short alley and started up the steps, walking quietly for no particular reason other than habit. Caught in a momentary wave of nostalgia, the girl, Salena, thought back three long years to when she had run away from home. She thought of the beatings and drunken lust of her father and of when she first sold her body to a man. She had been surprised at how many men, besides her paw, had hungered after the favors of a young girl. In the many months that passed since then, Salena thought with a tinge of cynical bitterness, she had lost the capacity to be surprised by anything. She sighed herself back to the present, and they continued to mount the stairs.

Across the street from them, in the other branch of the alley, a dark figure moved. Moonlight glinted, unseen, off the blued steel barrel of a Winchester while the silent watcher brought it into position and took careful aim.

When the sights centered on the middle of Pearly's back, a finger tightened on the trigger, and a fat blossom of yellow-orange fire grew at the muzzle, followed by the sharp report of the detonating cartridge.

Chapter 16

Pearly Wilson's back arched from the violent impact of the .44-40 slug that hit him half an inch left of his spine. The bullet ripped through muscle and nerves, plowing a widening tunnel through his lung and bursting his heart.

He smashed face first into the rough wooden steps and slithered down the stairway to land in a loose heap in the dirt. Salena stood where she had been when the shot came and screamed in shrill hysteria. Instantly the hidden assassin faded into the blackness of the alley. In the saloon, Riney and the gang reacted immediately.

"What the hell was that?" Charlie demanded, a glass of whiskey arrested in motion halfway to his mouth.

"A shot, stupid," Perk growled. His brow furrowed. "you don't suppose that li'l gal coulda put one into Pearly?"

Riney had risen and hurried to the front door. "Not Salena. That was a rifle." The girl's terrified shrieks could be clearly heard now. The gang leader stepped out onto the porch. "Don't just stand there chatterin'. Let's find out what happened."

They responded to Riney's command, rushing from

the saloon with their guns drawn. Salena continued to scream, providing a focus for their search. In short dashes from shadow to shadow, the men reached the opening between Howie's store and the millinery shop. Riney knelt beside Pearly's body.

"Charlie, Davey, go down that alley and take a look-see. Perk, go along this side of the street, check for any open doors. I'll look around here. He turned to Salena, whose shrill screeches had subsided to choked sobs. "An' you quit your cryin' and go get the doc." He took a closer look at Pearly. "Better make that the undertaker."

Salena remained unmoving, still sniffling and gulping. Riney raced up the stairs, two steps at a time, and shook her violently. "Snap out of it, girl. You ain't doin' him any good with that. Do what I said . . . right now!"

At last the terrified girl gained control of herself, nodded dumbly and walked past Riney, down the stairway and onto the street. Riney followed her partway and gave the area around Pearly's corpse a thorough search. In a few minutes the others returned.

"Well, whoever got him sure gave us the slip," Perk growled.

"Yeah. Who do you reckon it was, Riney?" Charlie added.

"How should I know, but I aim to find out. As of now, we got a town full of suspects. Let's get back to the saloon. That girl went for the undertaker."

"We gonna bury him in the mornin', Riney?"

Riney glowered at Charlie, his irritation fed by the uncomfortable knowledge that whoever had shot Pearly could as easily kill them all. "Don't ask fool questions, Charlie. Of course we'll bury Pearly in the morning.

We aren't gonna do it tonight."

Back at the saloon, the gang settled around a table and began to discuss likely suspects. Before they had discarded half a dozen names, the bat wings creaked open, and Miles Parrish entered, tall, black hat in hand.

"Ah . . . Mr. Stark?"

Riney scowled upward at the mortician. "What do you want?"

"I came in response to the young lady's request. I understand that misfortune befell one of your associates."

"If you mean some son of a bitch back-shot him, yeah. Now hear me good, buryin' man. We want the best funeral you got for him, and we want it at first light tomorrow morning."

Parrish was taken aback. He fumbled with his hat, and one hand strayed idly to his receding hairline to scratch a nonexistent itch. "Well, uh, sir, this is mighty short notice. I . . . my staff and I have certain preparations to make, you understand? And I need to know if there is a next of kin to notify. By the way, ah, who will pay the bill?"

Angered by the undertaker's vacillation, Perk leaped to his feet and thrust the muzzle of his Remington under Parrish's chin, then slowly drew back the hammer, a nasty grin spreading on his face.

"Don't you worry none about money, you damned vulture. The city of Colby's gonna provide for this funeral. And we do mean the very best you got. Any more objections from you and . . . *Szzzit!*" Perk drew his free hand slowly, ominously, across the undertaker's throat. "You follow me?"

Suppressed anger turned Miles's stomach to fire, but he managed to keep a calm expression while he nodded his assent. Perk released him and pushed the funeral director back, then gave him a light slap on the cheek.

"Then see that it's done up like the real thing."

A touch of sensible fear tempered the rage that Miles struggled to contain while he stalked to the door and made a quick exit. There was much to do, his mind worried, and who would he get this time of night to dig the grave and help him with the embalming?

Half an hour after sunrise the long, black, glass-sided hearse rattled to a stop outside the Idle Time Saloon. The gang, cleanly shaven and dressed in their best clothes, stepped onto the porch. Parrish fidgeted under their angry glowers and made a final check of his rig. He stepped up on the boardwalk and removed his hat. He had bad news to deliver, and he worried about the results of doing so.

"I . . . I'm sorry to say that the Reverend Brenski refused to conduct services or allow them to be held in his church. And Father O'Banyon is out of town delivering the last rites to a parishioner."

"We can dispense with that, Mr. Parrish," Riney told him in a quiet, reasonable tone. "Wouldn't surprise me if the walls fell in if Pearly got any churchin'. You can say a few words at the grave."

Relief lightened Miles Parrish's tense expression. He swallowed and produced a subdued smile. "I'll be glad to do so, Mr. Stark."

Miles popped his hat back on his head and took his place beside the driver of the hearse. The gang fell in behind, joined by Salena and two other saloon girls who wore somber black dresses, large hats with black veils, and solemn, haggard faces without makeup. The short procession wended its way along the main street of Colby toward the distant cemetery.

A mound of raw earth lay beside the deep oblong hole dug in one corner of Colby's nondenominational graveyard. Two ill-kept, bewhiskered men lounged nearby, leaning on the handles of their shovels. The hearse halted beside the open grave, and the gang served as pallbearers, placing Pearly's coffin on the lowering straps. Miles stepped down from the seat, removed his hat and produced a small, well-worn Bible. He crossed to the grave and cleared his throat, then looked upward at the pale blue sky.

"The Lord giveth and the Lord taketh away. Blessed be the name of the Lord. Oh, Lord, there was little we could do for this poor sinner here on Earth. George Thurmon Wilson, known to his friends of Pearly, led a violent life and was cut down in his prime by violence. Something got twisted up in him, and he strayed from your fold. Now we ask you to take him back and maybe do better by him than we did here. We thank You kindly. Amen."

The gang added their chorus of amens and self-consciously replaced their hats on their heads. Miles stepped over to Riney. "Ah, that will be forty dollars, Mr. Stark."

"Collect it from that fat-ass mayor of yours. We told you the city was going to pay for this funeral." Riney's eyes narrowed, an angry glint blazing from them. "Now, you got any idea who did this, Mr. Parrish?"

Miles bridled slightly. "My profession calls for me to

take care of the lamented remains of those who pass on, not to keep records of gunfights."

"Pearly weren't shot in no gunfight," Charlie growled. "He was bushwhacked. So why don't you just answer the question, mister? Do you or don't you know who kilt Pearly?"

Despite his personal courage, Miles recoiled from the gang's collective anger. He squeezed his eyes tightly shut, then opened them and spoke slowly, emphasizing each word:

"No. I do not know who shot your friend."

Charlie worked his thick, stained lips and spit a long stream of tobacco juice. "Well, why didn't you say that in the first place?"

Exasperation replaced Miles's momentary fear. "I *did* say that in the first place, you imbecile."

A puzzled look crossed Charlie's stupid face. "No you didn't. You started tellin' us what you did for a livin'."

"Leave it, Charlie," Riney commanded. "Let's get back and start roundin' people up. We got a lot of questions to ask."

Bells tolled mournfully over the town of Colby, and people stood, confused and a little frightened, in the yard outside Adam Brenski's church. More of the citizens arrived, herded by members of the gang. When Perk and Davey showed up with another group, they signaled Riney that everyone was now present. Riney climbed the steps to the sanctuary to where he could be seen and heard by all.

"All right, folks. Last night someone . . . one of you

. . . back-shot one of my men, Pearly Wilson. We aim to find out who it was. The guilty party can make it easy on everyone else if he just comes forward right now."

Behind Riney the door to the church opened, and an angry Adam Brenski stepped out. He held up his hands to the assembled citizens of Colby and called out loudly:

"All of you go home. You owe these men nothing."

"Just their lives, preacher," Riney drawled. "Which we can take from them at any time we damn well please."

"You would do well to take my warning to heart, Riney Stark," the minister replied ominously. "You can't intimidate an entire town. There aren't enough of you. You'd be wise to leave while you are still alive."

"What do you propose to do to stop us?"

"Never underestimate the power of the Lord," Adam Brenski said calmly.

"Bullshit!" Charlie snapped. "It weren't the Lord who plunked a forty-four-forty slug in Pearly's back, an' we're fixin' to find out who done it."

"That's right, preacher. These people are going to stand out here in the sun and sweat until we have an answer." Riney rapidly climbed the remaining two steps and violently rammed the muzzle of one .36 Navy Colt into Adam Brenski's stomach. Surprise blanked his face when, instead of doubling over in blue-faced agony, the preacher grunted slightly and a wild light came into his eyes. Before Riney realized its meaning, Adam Brenski swung a hard right that slammed into Riney's jaw, staggering him backward.

Riney didn't have time to react before Brenski hit

him two more times, a powerful left-right combination that drove Riney back against the church wall. Perk ran up behind the battling reverend and swung his Remington with all his strength.

The barrel made a solid, meaty sound when it struck Adam Benski's skull. The cleric sagged at the knees and fell in front of Riney Stark.

Riney viciously kicked Brenski, the force knocking him down the steps. "You son of a bitch!" Riney screamed, unable to control himself for the first time in his life. "All right, goddamn you," he yelled at the townspeople. "You'll stand out here until you die if we say so." He spun on one heel and strode angrily toward a table and chair set up under a nearby tree. Slowly his anger began to cool.

Two hours passed. The gang learned nothing more than they had when they assembled the townfolk. Howie stood among the crowd, one arm protectively around Amy's shoulders. She trembled slightly, her face ashen, and stared with glazed eyes at the men who had assaulted her. One by one, everyone in the gathering was questioned regarding his or her whereabouts the previous night, then returned to stand in the broiling heat. When it came Amy's turn, Howie guided her to a place before the table where Riney and Davey sat. The gang leader snapped his questions at the blank-faced woman, and she made strange, mewing sounds deep in her throat. Anger and protectiveness fired Howie to heated protest.

"Why don't you leave her alone? Haven't you men done enough harm to my wife? You can see she's not capable of anything right now."

"You might have a point there, storekeeper. Suppose

you tell us where *you* were? After we ran you and those other yokels off Main Street, I mean."

Howie hoped he could lie effectively. "I . . . I was home caring for Amy. She's . . . she's been like this ever since . . ." He let his words falter and stop.

"Yeah. It figures you'd not be up to even a bushwhackin'. You can go, storekeeper."

Howie led Amy from the churchyard, and none of the gang hindered their passing. He directed Amy's slow, aimless steps, cursing himself for his weakness and cowardice. When he got her home, he sat his wife in the living room and went to make a cup of tea. Behind him, Amy rocked and stared out window, a small, secret smile creasing her lips.

By noon the individual interrogations ended. Riney still knew nothing more about the shooting of Pearly Wilson. In frustration he ordered the crowd to disperse and led the way to the Idle Time. There each man downed a large, cool mug of beer. Then Riney sent his men out to make the daily collections. Any talk of leaving before they caught the killer had ended.

Late that night the gang sat around the table picking at plates of food. They had earlier run off the saloon girls and had the place to themselves. A moody silence pervaded the room, and the men ate methodically while slowly lowering the level of the bottles of whiskey on the green baize in front of them. Riney suddenly sat upright and snapped a bit of egg shell into a large brass spittoon.

"Damn, Charlie, whoever told you that you knew how to cook?" He lighted a long, slim cigar and took a deep puff before continuing. "We ain't gonna find out anything sittin' around here soakin' up booze. That killer is out there in this town someplace. All we gotta do is flush him out. I just got me an idea how we're gonna get him." Riney paused, the eyes of his men turned on him as tension built in the room.

"The fastest gun next to me in this outfit is Davey. I want him to go out there on the street and start walkin' patrol just like a real deputy. I want you to be real visible, Davey."

"You mean you expect me to walk around out there waitin' for some jasper to bushwhack me?"

Riney smiled, confident of the wisdom of his plan. "Not quite that, Davey. We won't be sitting here loafing until we hear the shot. We'll give you a couple minutes. Then we take to the rooftops along Main Street. If somebody even tries to stick his head out, he'll be covered six ways from Sunday."

Charlie blinked stupidly, an idiot's smile on his face. "That's a good idea, Riney."

"Sure it is, Charlie," Davey made sour reply. "If you're not the target."

"You want me to go, Davey? You want me, huh?"

"Shut up, Charlie. Here's how we'll work it," Riney continued. "Perk and I will cover this side, and Charlie, you cross over and watch the other."

Davey still looked a bit dubious. He downed his drink in a gulp and wiped his lips with the back of his hand. "Well, I sure hope it works like you say, Riney. If it don't, you'd better have Pearly move over."

Charlie immediately burst into wild laughter, holding his sides and letting tears roll down his chubby cheeks. Then he dried up quickly when he noticed the sober, disapproving looks of his three friends.

"Ready, Davey?"

"Might as well, Riney."

Davey got to his feet, loosened his Dragoon in its soft pouch holster and stalked to the door. He reached out with both hands to shove open the bat wings, only to have them blasted back into his face in a thousand splinters.

The hollow boom of a shotgun sounded from outside.

Chapter 17

Davey's body, driven by the charge of buckshot, flew back into the room and fell heavily on the sawdust-strewn floor. Nothing moved and no sound came for a stretched moment, then, with a protesting shriek, one bat wing door split at its hinges and dropped with a clatter. Through the opening the gang could see a human form, small in stature, half crouched in the street, reloading a shotgun.

"Look out!" Perk yelled when the assassin swung up the scattergun, and flame belched from one barrel.

Everyone ducked low, while bottles on the back bar shattered, spilling their contents, and the mirror behind them developed spiderwebs of crack-radiating holes.

"By God, I think it's that little feller from the store after all," Perk wondered aloud.

Another blast came from outside, followed by the sound of retreating footsteps. "Let's get him then," Riney commanded. "Charlie, lead the way."

"I-I c-can't, Riney. Really I can't. I'm skeered of

them things. Please don't make me go out there."

"All right, go out the back way, try to cut him off at the first corner. Perk, take the far side of the street. I'll go down this way."

Outside, on Main Street, they saw no sign of their ambusher. Perk crossed over, with Riney covering him, then started along the walk, his boots making a thunderous noise on the planks. Riney signaled him out into the street, then moved off himself. Both men reached the corner and joined up with Charlie. Still no hint of where the killer had gone. They heard a sound behind them, toward the Idle Time Saloon, and turned as one man.

The shotgun boomed again, harmlessly this time, and the dark-clad form disappeared into the blackness between two buildings. Perk started in that direction, but Riney stopped him with a hand on one arm.

"We won't get him this way. Let's go up to where he lives, cut him off at his house."

Riney led the way at a shuffling trot, up the first side street, through the next intersection, and at last stopped a hundred yards short of the small, white-painted clapboard house behind a low picket fence. He used silent arm signals to send Perk and Charlie to hiding places in the nearby shrubbery. The gang had an ambush of their own.

Half an hour passed without any sign of Howie Wilkins. He had not approached the house and no light nor activity had shown from within. Riney crept, hunched low, to where Charlie crouched behind a low privet hedge. He leaned close and whispered in Charlie's ear:

"Charlie, I want you to work your way around where

you can see both front and back doors. I'm going to get Perk and have him take the rear while I go in the front. One way or another we're gonna get to the bottom of this right now."

"Be careful, Riney. He's got that scattergun. Oh, Lordy how they scare me."

"That's why you're stayin' out here to watch the doors. When we get the drop on him, I'll call you in."

"Sure, boss. I'll be ready."

Riney moved on into the dark. He stopped by Perk and told him what to do. Then each went to his respective door. Riney heard Perk's nightingale whistle, counted three as arranged, then drew his sixgun and kicked in the front door. He dived through the opening, going low and to one side, the muzzle of his .36 Colt Navy out ahead of him. He waited a second, to the sound of tinkling glass from the kitchen and the solid bang of the rear door smashing against a wall. Then silence.

Riney's palms began to sweat, and he felt a vibrating tenseness in his body. He could imagine the muzzles of that side-by-side probing the darkness, seeking him, and wondered if Howie would light a lamp. His straining ears caught the sound of soft footsteps, and he nearly fired instinctively before he recognized the long, lanky form of Perk Perkins crouched in the doorway to the kitchen. With no response from their quarry, he had to do some planning.

From the outside shape of the building, Riney knew that the single bedroom would be off to his left, with a pantry or storage room behind that, off the kitchen, to complete the compact little square. He hissed to get Perk's attention.

"Over there," he whispered. "The bedroom."

Perk nodded and moved to one side of the door casing. Riney joined him. The door itself stood partway open. Bracing themselves they made ready. Riney reached out and around and shoved the thin wooden panel away from him. Rusty hinges creeked loudly in the dark, silent house, and Perk triggered off a nervous shot. No return fire followed his blast. At a nod from Riney they rushed into the room.

An empty bed lay before them, dimly illuminated by frosty starlight outside the window. Riney found a lamp and lit it, then called Charlie in from his post.

"D'ya git him?" Charlie asked excitedly.

"Naw," Perk drawled. "There ain't nobody here at all. The whole place is empty."

"How about that pretty li'l wife of his?"

"Gone, too, Charlie."

Riney added his own gloomy thoughts to the conversation. "It figures. He and his wife hid out somewhere in town. With only three of us we can never search the whole place effectively. They could always stay a block or two ahead of us and slip back in behind when we'd been through. We'll have to come up with some other way. Charlie, you go for that undertaker feller, Parrish, and meet us back at my room in the hotel."

"Sure, boss."

"I could use a drink, first," Perk admitted.

"Go snag one from the Idle Time and come on to the hotel. We got some heavy thinkin' to do between now and morning."

"Yeah," Perk said unhappily. "And another funeral to go to."

Miles Parrish's hearse rolled to a stop outside the Idle Time a short while after sunrise the next morning. Riney, Perk, and Charlie waited a few feet beyond the shattered bat wings. They wore their best clothes again and came out onto the porch with their hands on their gun butts. They looked about nervously and quickly formed behind the mortician's wagon. Miles said nothing and merely mounted to the driver's seat as the procession started out.

At the cemetery, beside the raw earth mound covering Pearly's grave, the hearse stopped at a new hole. It took the efforts of the gang, the undertaker, and his assistant to remove the rough pine coffin and prepare it for burial. The task completed, Riney, Perk, and Charlie removed their hats and stood at the graveside while Miles opened his Bible and cast a look heavenward.

"Lord, we're here again to send off to your keeping another strayed soul. Man is born in pain, lives but a brief while and is cut down in his prime, like the grain of the fields. Man has but a little time on this Earth . . . and bein' shot down from ambush *sure does* tend to shorten it. This is Davey Two-Knife, half redskin, half white. We commend his body to the ground and his soul to you. Ashes to ashes . . . dust to dust. Amen."

"That was right pretty, Mr. Parrish. I appreciate you puttin' that part about bein' ambushed," Riney said quietly while the casket was lowered into the grave.

"Well, he *did* pay right handsomely for the marshal's funeral. Figured he deserved something for that. That'll be forty dollars."

Anger flashed in Riney's eyes a moment. "Bill your

yellow-bellied mayor, Mr. Parrish." He spun on one heel and, followed by Charlie and Perk, stalked out of the cemetery.

Back at the Idle Time, the absolute silence of the town, the unnatural lack of any living being, outside the three outlaws, began to unnerve Riney and his men. Perk abruptly stood and hurled a half-full bottle, from which none of them had taken a drink, against the mirror. It sent what was left of the glass crashing into large, glittering shards.

"Damn it!" he cried. "Damn, damn, damn."

"Take it easy, Perk," Riney advised. "I would say we have definitely overstayed our welcome. We'd better hit that bank and get out of here while we still can."

"What about Pearly and Davey?" Charlie asked. "Are we goin' to let that little jasper get away with killin' 'em?"

"Do you have some bright idea how we're gonna find him without him finds us first?" Riney growled. "Charlie, you go to the livery and see our horses are made ready. Perk, you head over to the bank. Get 'em started puttin' the money into bags. I'll join you there in a few minutes."

"Right, boss." Perk hurried to the door, paused to look cautiously both ways before exiting, then stomped out onto the plankwalk.

Riney rose from the table. "Get movin', Charlie."

"Ah . . ."

"The back way if it makes you feel better. Just do it."

Perk Perkins walked rapidly along Main Street, glancing nervously into alleyways and hurrying past them. He crossed the intersection in a rush and headed at an angle toward the bank. He reached the midpoint of the street, avoided a large chuckhole, and looked up toward the entranceway. Then he felt a massive, tearing pain in his chest. A fraction of a second later he heard the blast of a shotgun. Perk cried out in agony and felt himself being lifted from his feet an instant before numb blackness closed over him.

Perk's body, flung to one side, struck the ground and sent up tiny billows of dust. In the distance Riney, who had only stepped onto the saloon porch a moment before the gunshot, dashed into the street in time to see a small puff of smoke drift away from the belfry of Brenski's church. He dashed forward, drawing his Colt and yelling for Charlie. His footsteps, pounding in the dust, sounded loud in his ears because of the utter silence throughout the town. He met Charlie in the intersection.

"What happened? I heard a shot."

"He got Perk, Charlie. From up there." Riney motioned toward the steeple. "We have him now, Charlie. We've got to take him."

"Is it the mercantile fellow or the preacher?" Charlie asked, confused.

Before Riney could reply, another blast came from the church, the pellets splattering harmlessly in the dust a few yards in front of the two outlaws. Charlie's eyes widened with horror.

"It don't matter, Charlie. We gotta get him, that's what counts."

Charlie hadn't heard Riney, his deep-rooted fear of

shotguns blanking out all but the reality of the weapon they faced. "You see that, Riney? That li'l feller's got a scattergun. I'm powerful skeered of them things, Riney, you know that."

"Listen, Charlie. He's trapped himself in there. We can get him now. You just do as I say."

Charlie's skin had taken on a pallid, green-white tinge. He plucked at Riney's sleeve while the two of them hurriedly crossed the street to the cover of intervening buildings.

"Aw, please, Riney. Don't make me go after him. I've always been afeared of them pellet guns."

"I told you what to do. We have a chance if you keep your head."

A third blast sounded from the steeple. The pellets ripped splinters from the building front a few feet over their heads. Charlie's eyes rolled wildly in their sockets while the wooden slivers drifted down around them. Almost as though talking to himself, Charlie began to ramble, his voice soft and pleading.

"My paw was shot with one of those things. I was just a little scamp, and I was right beside him. I got all splattered with his blood. It cut him in two, Riney, *in two*. I don't wanta get cut in two, Riney. I been scared of 'em ever since. Please, Riney, let's us just ride on out? I'm too scared to fight."

"Can it, Charlie!" Riney slapped Charlie's face, waited until the fat outlaw's eyes cleared. "We got us a chance to even the score for those boys, and we're gonna make good on it. *Then* we can ride out of this town with our heads high, not with our tails between our legs." He paused a moment to listen to the faint, distant sound of hurried footsteps that came from inside the tall belfry.

"He went down into the church, Charlie. Now we can rush the place."

Charlie turned frightened eyes on Riney, his voice a beggar's wail. "*It cut him in two*, Riney."

Riney's left hand flashed out, open palm, and again struck Charlie solidly on the cheek. The terrified outlaw's eyes lost focus a second, then steadied. "Charlie, snap out of it. We got him holed up in there."

"But that scattergun, Riney. He'll kill us both. I know it."

"Listen to me. He's in there, right? Now, he knows we're out front, and it stands to reason he'll be watching the front, you follow?"

"Yeah, Riney, sure."

"Then we can get him easy. You don't want to walk into that scattergun. I don't blame you for that. So we use a little strategy. We'll move up close to the church. You take this side, and I'll cut across the street, try to draw his fire. When we get up to that next corner there, I'll try to pin him down while you circle around and take him in the rear."

"But how, Riney? How?"

"There's a back door, dummy. All churches have a back door. All you got to do is get through it and throw down on him. Then I come in the front and we have him cold."

Understanding slowly dawned on Charlie. He lost some of his quavering fear, licked nervous lips. "Hey, yeah. By gosh I think so, Riney. Just like them *federales*. He-he-he."

Charlie surged forward then and advanced half a block down toward the church. He crouched low and fired a shot slantways through a front window. Then he rapidly blazed off three more when Riney ran diagonally across to the opposite side in line with him. Riney took up the fusillade while Charlie reloaded. The shotgun boomed once from a shattered window, and then silence returned to the streets of Colby. Riney motioned Charlie forward while he shot out the remaining windows in the front of the church.

Charlie rounded the corner into a side street, and Riney came quickly to his feet. He darted across Main Street, firing as he ran, to the better cover of the buildings there. Glass tinkled musically to the floor of the small white chapel, and then utter quiet held.

Riney took a prepared cylinder from the pouch on his belt and reloaded while he waited for Charlie to reach the back of the church.

Chapter 18

Charlie Bell pounded along the side street. His breath rasped loudly in his ears and, for a moment, he thought wildly of not turning off; of running on down to the edge of town and out onto the desert, away from the horror of the shotgun that awaited him in the church.

But Riney was counting on him.

He had to do what he could. He slowed at the first corner, hugged the building closely and peered around.

Not a soul on the street, not even a horse. No movement showed behind drawn blinds, and even the birds remained still.

Charlie cautiously crept around and started down toward a gap in the buildings, which indicated the back of the churchyard.

He made it halfway there and still nothing moved; no spray of agonizing shot smashed into his body. His stomach felt hollow, achingly empty. He advanced again, took even greater care. He reached the last concealing building and stopped to study the open expanse of ground, the fence, and gate.

Charlie stepped over the low pickets to enter the

yard, not trusting the gate not to speak and betray his presence. His palms sweated and the armholes of his shirt were stained darkly with moisture. He took a deep breath and ran, stumbling, to the back wall of the church.

Still no blast came to blow him into eternity. So far, so good.

He sidled along the wall to the door and put his hand on the knob.

It turned freely in his hand, and Charlie eased the door open a crack. He put his eye to the opening and peered inside. He could see nothing.

Charlie took a deep breath, slid the muzzle of his Remington through the gap and shoved harder.

His luck held.

Quickly he entered the small study off the sanctuary and closed the door behind him. On tiptoe he crossed the floor, bent low and duck-waddled out into the nave.

The pulpit blocked his view of the room, and he waited a while, listening. Shots sounded from outside, and the bullets smacked loudly into the wall separating the vestibule from the auditorium. Charlie took advantage of the distraction to jump out of hiding and dash down among the first rows of pews.

He ducked low among the stout-backed oak benches and caught his breath to listen again.

Nothing.

On hands and knees, Charlie edged along the pew toward the side aisle. Then he heard a board creak from behind him, over his left shoulder. He froze for an instant, then whirled and popped up, swung his Remington into line and let go a round.

The bullet struck the keyboard of an old pump

organ, blasted through and ripped a hole in the bellows. The ancient instrument gave off a tortured, ominous moan, and dust flew from its sprung wooden joints. From outside he heard Riney call to him.

"You all right, Charlie?"

"Yeah, Riney. Just shot me an organ."

Charlie continued to snake his way between the pews, eyes on the move to seek out his elusive prey. He worked himself halfway toward the rear and discovered he was blind to all sides. Charlie gathered his nerve and came up to his knees, peering around the embattled church.

He saw nothing and started to his feet. Fear and horror stabbed through him when he felt the cold steel circles press against the flesh of his neck.

He heard the hammers of the rabbit-ear shotgun ratchet back, and icy sweat popped out on his forehead. A moan of pure terror escaped his quivering lips, and he felt his legs go weak under him.

"Get up, you bastard," a voice behind the shotgun commanded.

It took some effort, but Charlie obeyed. His whole body shook with fear, and his mind refused to accept the evidence of his ears. The frigid steel muzzles probed again.

"Now, lay down that sixgun and turn around."

Charlie did as he was told, and his eyes widened with shock when all his senses verified what he had heard.

"Wha . . . what? It . . . it's *you*!"

"Yes, you raping son of a bitch," Amy Wilkins told Charlie. "It's me."

"Oh, please . . . please, ma'am. Put down that shotgun. I give up. Please don't point that thing at me."

"I'm going to do more than point it at you, you filth," Amy went on in a low, deadly purr. "I got the other three, now it's your turn."

"Oh, God, please not a shotgun. Use a knife, use anything . . . only don't, please don't shoot me with *that* thing."

Amy appeared not to hear his begging. "I'm going to make you pay for what you did to me. Then I'll take care of your fine Mr. Riney Stark."

Charlie began to sob in terror, great wet tears running down his cheeks, and he sank to his knees before the woman he had so gleefully raped only three days before. Amy stepped back a pace, brought the Greener to her shoulder, the muzzles pointing at Charlie's crotch.

"Charlie! You all right, Charlie?" Riney called from outside. He walked to the center of the street and called again. "Charlie?" When he received no reply he advanced into the churchyard and up the front steps. His hand reached for the doorknob.

Inside, the shotgun blasted. Its roar in the confined area drowned out Charlie's scream.

Riney jerked open the door and froze in horrified disbelief.

Massive shock had blessedly numbed Charlie's body and mind. He held himself upright by grasping the back of a pew and turned pleading eyes toward Amy.

The Greener blasted once more.

The top half of Charlie's head flew into the air in a shower of small bits and fine red mist. His body went rigid and then jacknifed awkwardly back over a pew. Amy turned to the door in the same moment Riney overcame his immobility and charged into the auditorium, swinging up his Colt.

"You're next, you bastard!" Amy screamed at him. She wheeled the long barrels into line and squeezed the trigger.

Riney stood open mouthed, eyes wide with stark horror for a solid, unmoving instant.

Then the firing pin of Amy's shotgun struck an expended cartridge.

Shock and surprise still rendered Riney helpless, but Amy screamed with rage and flung down the Greener. Her fingers contracting into sharp-tipped claws, she charged toward her last enemy.

From outside she heard the sound of angry voices and looked beyond Riney's shoulder to see a mob headed toward the church, led by her husband. The men were armed and determined. Two of them swung lengths of rope.

Riney heard them, too, turned away from the avenging woman and hurried outside onto the small stoop at the front of the church. He still had a loaded gun and meant to fight his way free or die in the attempt.

"Hold it right there, Stark," Howie Wilkins ordered, a new rumble of authority in his voice. On his vest his father's badge shined brightly in the morning sun. The crowd surged forward, but Howie raised a hand, stopping them.

"Throw down your gun, Stark. Your outlawing days are over."

The realization that Amy had been the unseen avenger finally struck Riney like a physical blow. He staggered slightly, then Amy tried to brush past him and go to her husband.

"Oh, Howard, I'm so proud of you," Amy cried out.

Then Riney Stark reached out with his free hand and grabbed her around the neck, drawing her in front of him.

"Nobody move or she dies! Back off, all of you. Get going or I'll blow off her head."

The mob of Colby citizens, growled in frustration but did as they were told. Riney Stark started down the steps, still holding Amy close. He advanced as the others retreated. When he reached the first intersection, he flung Amy toward her husband and ran frantically for the cover of a nearby alley. Immediately the angry mob took up pursuit.

"After him," Howard ordered. "Don't let him get away." He turned to Amy, who stood sobbing against his shoulder. "Why did you do it, Amy? How?"

"Oh, Howard, I thought . . . I believed you would never do anything to avenge what happened. I sat and rocked and thought about it until I couldn't stand it any longer. And when you didn't even come home after the final showdown with Stark and his men, I felt abandoned . . . ashamed and abandoned."

"Amy, my dear, dear Amy. We . . . we had to do something. We met in secret, laid plans to use dynamite, fire . . . anything to run Stark and his men out in the open where we could shoot them down from ambush. Then, when the first one got killed, we decided to wait and see, make more plans. I . . . I never dreamed it could have been you."

"I decided it was the only way. At least I could win back my self-respect, if not that of the town."

"Are . . . are you all right, dear?"

"Yes, Howard, now I am. And I'm so proud of you for taking the lead just now."

"Someone had to. Go on home. We have to hunt down Stark and put him in jail."

"Yes, husband. And . . . be careful, Howard."

Riney ran along the alley, paused at the cross street, then dashed on to the shelter of the buildings on the other side. Behind him he heard the sounds of pursuit. Like a fire-startled animal, confused and threatened, he dashed along for several more seconds before deciding on the livery. He changed direction and ran with purpose now, a definite goal in mind.

"There he goes," a voice called from behind. Riney stopped, spun in a low crouch and fired at the sound. A man screamed, clutched his chest and fell face first into the dusty street.

Riney ran on. The breath burned in his lungs, and he felt the blood pound at his temples. Sweat ran freely down his body, and he glanced around warily, ready for any more searchers he might encounter. He reached the livery to find it abandoned.

Time seemed to close in while Riney worked to saddle his horse. He tightened the cinch strap and tied it off, then swung down the left stirrup. He loosened the animal's reins and turned to lead him out of the stable. The figures of two men, armed with Winchesters, filled the wide doorway.

Riney's hand flashed to his Colt, and the first round detonated loudly the moment the muzzle cleared leather.

He didn't hit either man, hadn't planned to, only use the noise to startle them and get them off balance. His ploy worked, enough so that his second .36 caliber ball smacked into the brass side plate of the Winchester one man carried. It drove the townsman backward with a startled cry. Riney's Colt sounded a third time.

The round ball smashed bone and gristle in the other citizen's chest and exploded his heart. He reeled back and sideways into his partner, who stumbled and went to his knees. The remaining man tried to bring his rifle to bear, but failed to find his target when the outlaw sprang into the saddle and touched sharp spurs to his horse's flanks. The critter bolted forward, and Riney bent low to avoid the top of the door.

Out on the street he whirled in a dusty cloud of indecision for a second, then stretched out his pony into a rapid lope, heading in a direction he felt they would least expect him to take.

Behind him he heard startled shouts and curses, then Howie's voice, calm and forceful in command, ordering a posse to be formed.

Epilogue

Chunks of hard, red soil flew into the air, churned up by the ironshod hoofs of Riney's horse. He urged the stallion into a full gallop and thundered through the Mexican section of Colby in a swirl of dust. The peons, peering from the protection of their adobe houses, watched him with solemn eyes and crossed themselves in gratitude for his departure.

For his own part, Riney only wanted more speed.

He lashed his horse's flanks with the loose ends of his reins and gouged the animal's flanks bloody with his sharp spurs. The wind whistled past his ears and stung his eyes. Once clear of the last buildings of Colby, he turned aside and rode some distance behind the protecting spine of a low ridge.

The chase lasted for over an hour, with Riney at last giving the posse a false trail which they thundered off onto in blissful ignorance.

He rested his winded horse in the midst of a large cluster of boulders, one hand clamping the beast's nose to prevent it from calling out to the other animals when they rode by. In the near distance, Riney could see the windblown nags of the posse plodding along, heads down, like the hot, tired men who rode them. Riney remained silent and unmoving until they went far out of sight. At last he eased his tension and pushed back the brim of his Stetson with a thumb.

Calmly he rolled a cigar between his fingers, bit off the end and spit it out. A match flared when he struck it along the seam of his trousers and applied the flame to the cheroot. He puffed it to life and took a deep drag, then spoke out loud:

"It'll take a lot better men than that bunch to catch Riney Stark. Ah, but the price that was paid.

"Marv . . . an antsy kid, but a comer. Then Pearly . . . He rode with me a long time. Almost a real pard, old Pearly. I'll sure miss him. And Davey. Oh, Lord, they don't come any better than Davey.

"Perk? Well, Abner Perkins was different than all the rest. Don't suppose he'd ever ridden the owlhoot trail if things would have been all right when he came home from the war."

Riney took another drag, eyes alert on the wide horizon. He patted his horse's neck and affectionately scratched its ears, then gave a snort of laughter.

"Old Charlie was shit-scared to the end. The world ain't full of the likes of Charlie Bell and that's a blessing. But I'll miss him. Miss 'em all, for that matter, horse, ya hear?" Riney looked around again, satisfied himself he could move on in safety.

"Well, horse, it's time we made tracks." Riney led the animal out of the rocks and mounted.

He started off at a slow walk, letting the stallion have his head. When he came to the mouth of a high-walled canyon, which led off at right angles to the trail taken by the posse, he pulled on the left rein and headed his mount into the shade-dark entrance. Riney smiled to himself and looked back over his shoulder at the vast, empty expanse of desert and, in the distance, a soft blue haze over the town of Colby.

"Yep," he spoke aloud again, "those townies sure can't track worth a damn." He felt a great weight lifting from him. "Hell, I can always start over. Build a new gang." He suddenly laughed aloud.

"No matter, I'm free and away now for sure. And there's all that silver buried in Mexico. There'll be better days." Riney turned to the front and halted abruptly, his face going blank with shock and uncertainty. Hesitantly, slowly to insure no one misunderstood the gesture, he raised one hand, palm outward, and smiled nervously.

"You friends? I . . . er . . . I come in peace."

Natana-jo sat unmoving astride his pony, his face a grim mask.

The silence stretched agonizingly for Riney. No one moved, and he felt the sweat trickle from his armpits and down between his shoulder blades. It seemed to be made of ice water. At last the Apache chief jerked his head to one side in silent command.

Two Apaches slipped from their mounts and came to Riney's side. They reached up and dragged him from the saddle. He struggled hopelessly with them while they pulled him to a place before the war chief. A smile of satisfaction spread on the Apache leader's lips.

"We have waited a long while for this, white-eye," *Natana-jo* said in his own language. Around him the other braves nodded and smiled in wicked anticipation. *Natana-jo* swung a leg over his horse's withers and dropped lightly to his feet. Metal hissed against leather when he drew his long-bladed knife.

"We will grow strong from your spirit." He advanced on Riney, whose eyes had grown wide with terror.

Riney Stark's first scream echoed off the high walls of the canyon, startled birds from their perches and continued to bounce back and forth. Then he shrieked again . . . and again.

The screams lasted a long time. *Natana-jo* made sure of that.

THE UNTAMED WEST
brought to you by Zebra Books

THE LAST MOUNTAIN MAN (1480, $2.25)
by William W. Johnstone
He rode out West looking for the men who murdered his father and brother. When an old mountain man taught him how to kill a man a hundred different ways from Sunday, he knew he'd make sure they all remembered . . . THE LAST MOUNTAIN MAN.

SAN LOMAH SHOOTOUT (1853, $2.50)
by Doyle Trent
Jim Kinslow didn't even own a gun, but a group of hardcases tried to turn him into buzzard meat. There was only one way to find out why anybody would want to stretch his hide out to dry, and that was to strap on a borrowed six-gun and ride to death or glory.

TOMBSTONE LODE (1915, $2.95)
by Doyle Trent
When the Josey mine caved in on Buckshot Dobbs, he left behind a rich vein of Colorado gold—but no will. James Alexander, hired to investigate Buckshot's self-proclaimed blood relations learns too soon that he has one more chance to solve the mystery and save his skin or become another victim of TOMBSTONE LODE.

GALLOWS RIDERS (1934, $2.50)
by Mark K. Roberts
When Stark and his killer-dogs reached Colby, all it took was a little muscle and some well-placed slugs to run roughshod over the small town—until the avenging stranger stepped out of the shadows for one last bloody showdown.

DEVIL WIRE (1937, $2.50)
by Cameron Judd
They came by night, striking terror into the hearts of the settlers. The message was clear: Get rid of the devil wire or the land would turn red with fencestringer blood. It was the beginning of a brutal range war.

Available wherever paperbacks are sold, or order direct from the Publisher. Send cover price plus 50¢ per copy for mailing and handling to Zebra Books, Dept. 1934, 475 Park Avenue South, New York, N.Y. 10016. Residents of New York, New Jersey and Pennsylvania must include sales tax. DO NOT SEND CASH.

GREAT WESTERNS
by Dan Parkinson

THE SLANTED COLT (1413, $2.25)
A tall, mysterious stranger named Kichener gave young Benjamin Franklin Blake a gift. It was a gun, a colt pistol, that had belonged to Ben's father. And when a cold-blooded killer vowed to put Ben six feet under, it was a sure thing that Ben would have to learn to use that gun—or die!

GUNPOWDER GLORY (1448, $2.50)
Jeremy Burke, breaking a deathbed promise to his pa, killed the lowdown Sutton boy who was the cause of his pa's death. But when the bullets started flying, he found there was more at stake than his own life as innocent people were caught in the crossfire of *Gunpowder Glory*.

BLOOD ARROW (1549, $2.50)
Randall Kerry returned to his camp to find his companion slaughtered and scalped. With a war cry as wild as the savages', the young scout raced forward with his pistol held high to meet them in battle.

BROTHER WOLF (1728, $2.95)
Only two men could help Lattimer run down the sheriff's killers—a stranger named Stillwell and an Apache who was as deadly with a Colt as he was with a knife. One of them would see justice done—from the muzzle of a six-gun.

CALAMITY TRAIL (1663, $2.95)
Charles Henry Clayton fled to the west to make his fortune, get married and settle down to a peaceful life. But the situation demanded that he strap on a six-gun and ride toward a showdown of gunpowder and blood that would send him galloping off to either death or glory on the . . . *Calamity Trail*.

Available wherever paperbacks are sold, or order direct from the Publisher. Send cover price plus 50¢ per copy for mailing and handling to Zebra Books, Dept. 1934, 475 Park Avenue South, New York, N.Y. 10016. Residents of New York, New Jersey and Pennsylvania must include sales tax. DO NOT SEND CASH.

THRILLING FICTION
from Zebra Books

THE LEADER AND THE DAMNED (1718, $3.95)
by Colin Forbes
Only Martin Bormann knew the truth of Hitler's death until Ian Linsey stumbled onto the incredible deception. Now the gestapo is out to capture him and torture him to death because he holds the knowledge that Hitler is a fake.

FIREFIGHT (1876, $3.95)
by Richard Parque
For Marine Captain Montana Jones, the war was over . . . until the cablegram arrived from 'Nam that said, "Please help me!" Montana knew he had to go back to find the raven-haired wife he thought was dead . . . to rescue her from the Cong in one final blood-drenched FIREFIGHT.

DEADLY ERNEST (1909, $3.95)
by Daniel Lynch
Lt. Murphy had never seen a woman as brutally beaten as the murder victim just a few blocks from his home. It looked like a random killing which meant it would happen again—and again—until Murphy caught the killer, or the killer caught him.

HIGH COMMAND (1910, $3.95)
by Anton Emmerton
As Great Britain falls to the Communist tanks, Ex-British Intelligence agent, John Sulley, must mount a daring commando raid on the isolated hideout of the Supreme Commander of the Soviet forces.

BLOODLAND (1926, $3.95)
by William W. Johnstone
America's farmbelt had changed, and Key Lessard knew he would have to go to war again—only this time against a secret army of his own countrymen, against a neo-Nazi army of vengeance and hate.

Available wherever paperbacks are sold, or order direct from the Publisher. Send cover price plus 50¢ per copy for mailing and handling to Zebra Books, Dept. 1934, 475 Park Avenue South, New York, N.Y. 10016. Residents of New York, New Jersey and Pennsylvania must include sales tax. DO NOT SEND CASH.

THE SURVIVALIST SERIES
by Jerry Ahern

#1: TOTAL WAR	(0960, $2.50)
#2: THE NIGHTMARE BEGINS	(0810, $2.50)
#3: THE QUEST	(0851, $2.50)
#4: THE DOOMSAYER	(0893, $2.50)
#5: THE WEB	(1145, $2.50)
#6: THE SAVAGE HORDE	(1232, $2.50)
#7: THE PROPHET	(1339, $2.50)
#8: THE END IS COMING	(1374, $2.50)
#9: EARTH FIRE	(1405, $2.50)
#10: THE AWAKENING	(1478, $2.50)
#11: THE REPRISAL	(1590, $2.50)
#12: THE REBELLION	(1676, $2.50)

Available wherever paperbacks are sold, or order direct from the Publisher. Send cover price plus 50¢ per copy for mailing and handling to Zebra Books, Dept. 1934, 475 Park Avenue South, New York, N.Y. 10016. Residents of New York, New Jersey and Pennsylvania must include sales tax. DO NOT SEND CASH.

DEPTH FORCE
by Irving Greenfield

Built in secrecy, launched in silence, and manned by a phantom crew *The Shark* is America's unique submarine whose mission is to stop the Russians from dominating the seas. There's no room for anything other than victory or death, and the only way to stay alive is to dive deep and strike hard.

DEPTH FORCE	(1355, $2.95)
#2: DEATH DIVE	(1472, $2.50)
#4: BATTLE STATIONS	(1627, $2.50)
#5: TORPEDO TOMB	(1769, $2.50)
#6: SEA OF FLAMES	(1850, $2.50)
#7: DEEP KILL	(1932, $2.50)

Available wherever paperbacks are sold, or order direct from the Publisher. Send cover price plus 50¢ per copy for mailing and handling to Zebra Books, Dept. 1934, 475 Park Avenue South, New York, N.Y. 10016. Residents of New York, New Jersey and Pennsylvania must include sales tax. DO NOT SEND CASH.